THE EROTIC ODYSSEY OF COLTON FORSHAY

By

James H Longmore

A HellBound Books Publishing LLC Book
Austin TX

James H Longmore

**A HellBound Books LLC
Publication**
Copyright © 2021 by HellBound Books Publishing LLC
All Rights Reserved

Cover and art design by Kevin Enhart for
HellBound Books Publishing LLC

Edition 2

**No part of this book may be reproduced, stored in a retrieval system, or
transmitted by any means, electronic, mechanical, photocopying, recording
or otherwise without written permission from the author
This book is a work of fiction. Names, characters, places and incidents are
entirely fictitious or are used fictitiously and any resemblance to actual
persons, living or dead, events or locales is purely coincidental.**

www.hellboundbookspublishing.com

Printed in the United States of America

BY JAMES H LONGMORE

HORROR
Blood & Kisses
'Pede
Tenebrion
Flanagan

BIZARRO
The Erotic Odyssey of Colton Forshay
Buds
And Then You Die
Feeder
I Am Joe's Unwanted Penis

James H Longmore

THE EROTIC ODYSSEY OF COLTON FORSHAY

James H Longmore

CHAPTER ONE

It was raining bodily fluids again; only this time it was semen. Colton Forshay hunkered down, his head against the upturned collar of his beige trench coat and cursed himself that he'd been foolish enough to venture outside at this time of the year without an umbrella. Although, he placated himself, this inclement weather was preferable to the menstrual blood downpour they'd had last week. That thick drizzle had consisted of clotted blobs of stale, rancid blood, which had totalled his favorite coat, hence the new one he was sporting this particular afternoon.

Colton trudged onward and found himself counting the steps to his neighbor's house, an old habit from his childhood. As he walked, he tried his level best to ignore the fat gobbets of seminal fluid that spattered on him from the heavens to mat his hair and make the sidewalk slippery and incredibly dangerous to walk on. Step by step, he began to wish he'd stayed home, and found himself not really relishing the idea of standing around and making with the small talk at the O'Keefes' neighbourhood barbecue—certainly not in this hellish weather. Having said that, at least the O'Keefes had a gazebo; Tom had put it up the previous year after the diarrhea showers had ruined their *Back to School* family barbecue (why *did* those people always have to have a theme?) It wasn't like it was a capital crime to have a theme-less barbecue with family and friends *just because.*

Not anymore, it wasn't; that particularly arcane law had been repealed shortly after the great tartan shortage of '98 that led to a dearth of slutty, schoolgirl outfits. Yep, those days were long gone.

The sickly, seminal smell of the stuff that adhered to his coat was making Colton feel more than a little queasy, and he desperately wanted to breathe through his mouth to quieten the nausea that arose in his gullet. He'd discovered early in life that taking big, deep gulps of air worked wonders to stave off the urge to vomit; it had something to do with giving the brain something else to think about other than antiperistalsis. It was not so much that Colton was averse to throwing up, but he did prefer it to be on his terms—when *he* wanted to and upon who he chose. But, despite the growling sickness that rumbled in the pit of his gut, Colton kept his mouth clamped firmly shut. The last thing he wanted was a mouth full of cum to complement the bile at the back of his throat and make his tongue go numb.

Only a hundred yards or so to go, he told himself, *almost there.* Colton could see the O'Keefe's gaily painted front door from there; a gaudy, neon yellow snuggled between two unruly sage bushes that always reminded Colton of the pubic hair of those crudely drawn couples in 1970s sex manuals.

It had been Barbara O'Keefe who had slid the invitation to the barbeque (she'd abbreviated it *BBQue,* which Colton had thought quaint) under Colton's front door on Thursday just after lunch. He'd watched her scurry away down his pathway, having ignored her insistent knocking for what seemed an excessive amount of time; he'd not been in much of a mood for chatty neighbors that afternoon, no matter how alluring they looked naked. And it had to be said, the nude Barbara O'Keefe on his driveway had really cheered up his otherwise humdrum Thursday. He'd kept his eyes on Mrs. O'Keefe from behind his net curtains until she was safely out of sight. He'd been particularly mesmerized by the sway of her huge, pendulous breasts, even though they were marred by a myriad of stretch marks that made them look like a map of the Amazon tributaries. She'd only squeezed out one kid, and her tits were all shot to hell and back. *It sure was a cruel, cruel world*, thought Colton. She had been wearing the purple strap-on as she often did on her forays outdoors, and Colton saw clearly the tight leather straps dug harshly into her tanned, ample flesh to chafe it in places. The erect dildo attached by the straps had waggled gaily in front of her as she walked, like some oversized, phallic divining rod. Colton deduced the strap-on she was wearing was the one with the remote, vibrating protuberances on the inside that Tom O'Keefe had bragged about what seemed like a lifetime ago.

"There's one up inside her vag', and one on the clit." Tom had guffawed to the Forshays, much to Alicia's delight, as Colton recalled with a little sadness. And, by the way Barbara O'Keefe skipped in her step every now and then as she sashayed down the street on those impossibly high heels—six inches at the very least. Colton figured Tom had been sitting at home pressing the remote button like a mad thing to get his wife all wet and unnecessary.

Last minute invitation or not, afterthought or otherwise, it really didn't matter much to Colton. It wasn't as if he had anything to do, or any place to be. That had been his lot in life since Alicia had been murdered on the TV show. All of

Colton's neighbors knew just how much he missed his wife, how much they had lived for each other, and had steered clear of the erstwhile life-and-soul of every block party. In fact, the invitation from the O'Keefes was the first one he'd had in over a year. Perhaps they figured his time for mourning should be over and done with, and it was time to face the Alicia-less world.

Especially once word had gotten out about Eric's birth.

It would always be a mystery to Colton as to how he'd actually managed to get his dog pregnant. It wasn't as if he'd taken it anywhere to meet other dogs, he himself had always taken precautions, *and* he'd had the thing neutered. Oh yeah, and it had been a boy dog too!

But, to Colton's surprise, Jethro the boxer/German shepherd cross had wound up in the family way; his broad flanks swelled by the day for about three months or so, when out popped Eric.

Jethro had run off shortly after the birth, left a note about needing some space to think that was pretty much *'I'm off for good, sucker'* between the lines, and left Colton to raise Eric alone.

Look on the bright side, Colton invoked his mantra; at least what he was going through wasn't quite as bad as the guy at number three-o-eight who'd gotten his 2006 Chevy Cobalt pregnant. At least Eric looked a bit like Colton and could play Yahtzee and engage in good conversation.

Since receiving the invite, Colton had hummed and hawed for all of the two days following as to his potential attendance. He was not so sure if he was up to putting himself through the niceties of his neighbors' sympathy and their disapproving looks as they would inevitably ask how Eric was getting on. But the handwritten invitation had informed that this year's O'Keefe barbecue was in honor of their daughter, Julie, and this had piqued Colton's interest insomuch as he simply couldn't believe the slip of a gal who used to dog sit for he and Alicia had come of age.

Whilst it would be *nice*, he supposed, to catch up with his neighbors and get his first post-Alicia's death social gathering out of the way, Colton had thought it would be good to see how Julie O'Keefe had filled out over the past year or so.

As it turned out, Colton had actually misread the invitation. In some way, it served him right for eschewing the reading glasses he pretended not to need. The O'Keefe's barbecue party was not in honor of their daughter, Julie. It was, in fact, a barbecue *of* their *honored* daughter, Julie.

They were just finishing up pulling out her teeth when Colton arrived.

"Oh, hi, Mr. Forshay." Julie greeted him as she sat up in the faux-rattan garden chair. Her voice affected a sibilant lisp caused by the lack of front teeth, which lay like bloodied popcorn on the glass-topped table in front of her. As she spoke, her voice as cheerful as Colton remembered it from her dog-sitting days, was bright and breezy. Bright, frothy blood bubbled from her mouth as she spoke and dribbled down her chin, adding to the spreading crimson stain on the front of her flimsy white nightgown.

As he said his hello, Colton saw Julie already had her finger and toenails pulled out, as tradition dictated; the bloody, ragged stumps of her fingers splashed blood as she waved at him.

"Hey, Colton!" Tom O'Keefe called over. "Glad you could make it!" He waved Colton a greeting, bloodied pliers in hand. The guy holding her down by the shoulders, who Colton recognized as Aiden Venegas from number sixty-two, didn't look up; he seemed distracted by Julie's nipples that were prominent and most noticeable through the blood-stained gown.

Colton nodded hello back, peeled off his bejizzed coat, and handed it to the ever-attentive Barbara O'Keefe, who had appeared at his side as if by magic the second he'd arrived. Colton took note that today she was *sans* strap-on. In fact, she was *sans* anything at all, and her naked skin was slick and glistened with atmospheric ejaculate from running in and out of the house to attend to her guests.

A cursory look around the party and Colton figured everybody who was anybody in the neighborhood was there. He guestimated twenty-ish people in all and a handful of assorted animals. The party guests—the human ones—all stood around making polite chitchat, waiting patiently for the cooking to begin.

Of the people Colton knew on terms more than a polite nod in the street, there was Venegas, although his morbidly obese wife was conspicuous by her absence. Elizabeth Venegas hadn't set foot outside of their house in three or four years now, to Colton's recollection; she'd simply gotten too damn big. There were the Flynns from one-two-seven, the Greens who lived just across the road from Colton's house; he'd watched them fuck many a time as their bedroom window faced his. Patricia had a penchant for taking David's not insubstantial dick anally with her breasts mashed up against the window pane. Colton had an inkling they knew full well he watched them, cock in hand; it was more than possible the show was as much for his benefit as it was theirs. Patricia grinned and tipped Colton a sly wink as he walked by them to grab himself a glass of the O'Keefe's famous fruit punch.

He smiled at George McLaughlin who grinned back with yellowed, crooked teeth. George was about a billion years old and had lived alone on the street since his wife passed away twenty-three years ago. He'd not remarried and preferred instead to spend his time—and considerable savings—on the prostitutes who frequented his home twice a week. The neighbors didn't seem to mind, and no one said anything to old George, even though the hooker's pimps would hold their vigils outside his house for anywhere between a half hour and sunup (dependent upon George's stamina and erectile dysfunction drug intake on the day), or that the girls he picked out seemed to be the most dishevelled, haggard specimens the internet had to offer. Colton avoided George's attempt to start up a conversation and squeezed by pretending to be on his way to join the Woolstons who were busy nibbling on celery sticks and glancing over in his direction with *that* pitying look on their faces. Colton raised a finger at George as if to say *I'll be back to chat later, old friend*, although the gesture meant nothing of the sort. Given the choice, Colton decided he would prefer to listen to Cole and Honey-Lou Woolston's tales of a sex life extraordinaire than to exchange dead wife stories with George McLaughlin; especially since George's wife had died peacefully in her sleep and not screaming in agony on a syndicated TV show.

Like Mrs. O'Keefe, Honey-Lou Woolston wore very little as a matter of habit, much to the delight of everyone fortunate to know her. Although, whilst the exposure of so much skin was most appealing at these shindigs, Colton had been pleased to note upon arrival that not everyone at the O'Keefe's party was in a state of undress; the majority of the guests had chosen to dress smart-but-casual. In ironic contrast to his wife, Mr. Woolston wore beige slacks, deck shoes, and a pale-pink polo.

The exhibitionist element, thus far, was restricted to Barbara, Honey-Lou Woolston, and Joe Sonemaly; the latter of which was on hands and knees fellating the Very Reverend Smallwood whilst being fucked in the ass by the O'Keefe's miniature Shetland pony. As the pony thrust into him, Joe's genitals dangled like a hypnotist's watch in a small nettle patch, which was stinging his scrotum into a red, swollen mess. Colton smiled over at the unholy trio. *Shame on Tom and Barbara*, he thought; *they really ought to do something about their weed problem.*

Colton returned his attention to Honey-Lou Woolston. She was always a favorite at these neighborhood gatherings. It was not, it had to be said, just for her inherent dislike of clothing, but also for her winsome wit and eagerness to screw anyone and anything once the inevitable orgy started up. Honey-Lou had the most fantastic body in the district; slim, lithe with well-defined abdominal muscles, her skin tanned to a honey-gold with—of course—no tan lines. Her neat breasts were of just the right proportions, and her body was completely devoid of hair from her immaculately epilated pudendum to her cue-ball smooth head. Since pubic hair had been declared illegal, some such as Honey-Lou had taken the law to the extreme and chose to remove every strand of hair they possessed. The downside of this was that it had led to the dubious underground movement of hirsute folk, along with niche 'hairy' porn, and a burgeoning black market in bush wigs.

"Hello, Colton," Honey-Lou said. Her husky voice caused his dick to twitch a little. "It's been far too long." She smiled at him.

"Sure has, buddy." Cole Woolston grinned and slapped Colton firmly on the shoulder. "We've all missed you and Alicia." Honey-Lou dug a well-honed elbow into her husband's ribs, and her tits wiggled at Colton.

"It's okay," Colton told them as his eyes involuntarily cast their gaze downward.

He couldn't help but stare. Honey-Lou wore nought but fine, gold chains—most likely eighteen carat, Colton guessed. They hooked onto her looped nipple rings and spread down in a twinkling fan shape to her vagina. There, they were attached to fine hooks that spiked through her inner and outer labia and stretched taut to pull her open. The vivid pink flash of her vulva yawned like a gaping, fleshy mouth. Colton could see quite clearly that Honey-Lou's distorted sex was oozing wet in its state of arousal, her vagina an open black hole. In her exposed pee-hole, Honey-Lou had inserted a solid gold rod that sported a diamond-encrusted ball that twinkled brightly against the moist, inviting flesh. Colton knew the urethral plug went inside as far as the bladder, as was the fashion of the day, and prevented urination. As a result of this intrusion, Honey-Lou's lower belly appeared slightly distended, and Colton thought she really ought to ease up on the wine, as delicious as it was.

"Hey, Colton!" It was Tom O'Keefe's voice that broke Colton's contemplation of the delicious Mrs. Woolston's genitalia. Not that Honey-Lou or her husband would be minding in the least that Colton stared; in fact, they would have been offended if no one did considering the effort Honey-Lou had gone to. Why else would she dress in nothing and spread her cunt out like that? Give their encounter another five minutes, and as Colton recalled from previous times, Cole would be inviting him to slip a finger or two—or three—into Honey-Lou's unguarded vagina and bring her to one of her trademark ear-splitting climaxes.

Colton turned around and saw Tom beckoning him over.

"Please excuse me," he said to the Woolstons. "Let's catch up later?"

"Sure thing, sexy dick," Honey-Lou purred. She tugged on her chains to stretch her pussy even wider, like she was some bizarre, erotic puppeteer, and Colton's dick twitched once more.

Colton made his way over to Tom, weaving through the party guests while murmuring hellos to smiling faces he'd not clapped eyes on since Alicia was alive.

"Thought we'd let the guest of honor do the honors." Tom O'Keefe grinned and handed over a long, thin metal spike that was an easy six feet long. Colton twirled the spike around in his hands enjoying the feel of the cool, smooth metal in his hands. He caught his reflection in the shining steel and saw the honed point at the business end glinted in the yellow light of the flames from the newly lit firepit.

Colton looked down at Julie O'Keefe, who now lay on her stomach on a plastic sheet that had been hastily spread over the rough concrete floor. David Green, husband to the wife with the window-breasts, held Julie's shoulders down whilst Aiden Venegas and the long-haired guy from the *Ye Olde Smoke Shop* each gripped one of her pale, slender feet to hold her legs apart. The girl's firm, rounded rump was raised in the air, her bloodied face pressed hard on the ground.

"Hello again, Mr. Forshay." Julie's voice was distorted through bloody, swollen gums. "I hope you're having a good time," she said.

"When you're ready, Colton." Tom ushered his guest, who had no idea he was actually the guest of honor at this party, to the rear end of his daughter. Tom gripped Julie's buttocks firmly and spread her cheeks wide apart and Colton saw the crinkled hole of her anus relax a little.

Tom gave Colton a go-ahead nod.

Colton studied the girl at his feet as she lay there perfectly still to await her fate. Her milky, smooth skin glistened in the fire light; the streaks of dried blood from her torn nail beds, and those around her delightful, full-lipped mouth somehow added to the allure of her young body. She looked beautiful.

Colton readied the skewer and eased it into Julie's perfect, puckered anus—bleached especially for the occasion—slowly but firmly pushed against the tightness of her sphincter muscle.

Julie squirmed a little as the cold metal penetrated her body and moaned softly as it slipped inside her. Colton knew from experience this was the part that was pleasurable.

Around eight inches or so into Julie's body, Colton felt a slight resistance as the skewer reached the end of her rectum—hence her body's natural corridor—and began to ease itself through the wall of her bowel. Julie let out a little cry and wriggled against the strong hands that held her in place. Bright, scarlet blood trickled out from the girl's ass and made snaking rivulets down her thighs.

Undeterred, Colton continued on. He leaned his weight into the skewer and kept his hand steady to maintain an even forward thrust. Julie began to moan a little louder this time, and Patricia Green joined the skewering party to stroke the girl's hair and make soothing noises.

By this time, most of the party guests were gathered around, eyes wide and sparkling with marvel at the spectacle by the fire pit. This was, after all, the highlight of the evening.

Julie writhed, trying her very best to be brave and to work against the agonizing pain that tore through her body. At around eighteen inches in, the blood oozing from Julie's violated ass bubbled out mixed with fecal matter from her ruptured bowels. It created a muddy looking, thick fluid that dripped thickly from between her buttocks. Someone stepped forward. Colton thought he recognized the guy from a previous party but was damned if he could put a name to the face. The party guest placed a metal bowl between the girl's trembling legs to catch the mixture. The bowl was already half filled with Julie's pee and menstrual blood that had been collected earlier, and the fouled liquid drip-dripped in and turned it cloudy. The smell from the bowl, and from Julie's ass, made Colton's eyes water and his stomach heave for the second time that day. The contents of the bowl, he knew, would be used as a marinade once the barbecue finally got under way, although that did little to ease his tightening guts.

About a third of the way along the skewer, a little over twenty-four inches into its journey inside Julie O'Keefe, Colton felt more resistance. If his high school biology served him right, and if he had stayed true with the spike, he had reached the girl's cardiac sphincter at the top of her stomach.

He leaned into the skewer and pushed hard.

Julie tensed all of her muscles as the spike thrust through her stomach and deep into her heart. She gripped David Green's arms tight with her blood smeared hands.

"*Bon appetit*," Julie said as their eyes met, and she slipped away with a guttural grunt and a cough of thick blood.

As Julie's body slumped to the floor, Colton finished up his job and continued the skewer on and up until it emerged through her mouth. He pushed until a clear twelve inches or so protruded from her slack, toothless jaw.

Afterward, Colton helped Tom, Aiden, and David hoist Julie's limp body onto the spit above the fire pit. As he lifted, amazed at just how heavy the girl's slight body was, he remembered something he'd read about spit roasts. In England, a spit roast was where two soccer players, usually premier league, got some ditzy blonde chick drunk in a hotel room and fucked her at both ends at the same time. Colton had also read there was usually a mutual, premiership high-five, and much joshing between the players during proceedings.

Here, it was more literal.

"You did a good job there, Colton." Aiden Venegas slapped Colton on the back and handed him a freshly cracked beer. "You really *must* come over to ours next Sunday. Elizabeth and me are having one of our parties." He beamed.

Colton nodded and cast his mind back to past parties at the Venegas's place. As obese as that woman was, Lizzie Venegas sure knew how to entertain her guests come party time. So, Colton agreed that he would come along, and Aiden seemed delighted.

In spite of his initial reticence, Colton found he was actually enjoying himself. In fact, now that he was back in the swing of things, he was feeling quite sociable. It could have been the beer, being back among the old crowd, or the successful skewering, but Colton began to think that yes, perhaps it was high time he did get back into circulation.

***

In a throwback tradition to caveman days, the menfolk gathered around the firepit to admire the slowly rotating corpse of Julie O'Keefe and exchange chitchat punctuated with chugging at cold beer. Tom O'Keefe kept the spit turning with expert ease, pausing only to ladle the thick basting mix over his daughter's crackling, hissing body. The heady, meaty, metallic aroma rose high and drifted temptingly around the party and surrounding neighborhood, whetting appetites, and making stomachs rumble.

A late arrival pushed his way through the gathering, his face red with exertion and hair matted with sweat and seminal fluid.

"I'm so sorry I'm late." He apologized to Barbara with a kiss on her cheek and a sly grope of her bare ass.

"That's okay, Geoff." Barbara assured him with a saucy smile. "As long as you brought the wine."

Colton kind of half-recognized Geoff Barlow. He was a history teacher at the local high school; they'd crossed paths at neighborhood parties a handful of times in the old days. Geoff thrust a bottle clad in a brown paper bag at his hostess.

"You have no idea what I had to pay to get this," Barlow panted as he ran his hand through his slick hair. "The liquor store guy's wife wanted *triple* penetration, and so I had to wait around for the other guy to turn up." He gave a flustered smile. "I did suggest we use the baseball bat they keep behind the counter but nooooo—" Barlow grabbed at his crotch for emphasis. "She had to have the real thing!"

"I'm sure it was worth it." Barbara rubbed her erect nipples against Barlow's arm. "I hear this one is a particularly good vintage."

"It had better be," Barlow said. "Pushing my dick into a pussy with two others has given me hellish friction burns. I mean, she was loose, three kids I believe, but not *that* fuckin' loose." Barlow laughed out loud.

"Well, thank you for making that sacrifice, Geoff," Barbara cooed. "I'll make sure you are justly rewarded." She winked. "I guess you may be excused from making the barbecue contribution this time around."

"Wouldn't dream of it, Mrs. O'." Barlow grinned and fished out a massive, if not somewhat red and chafed, cock from his unbuttoned pants. Barbara looked down at it and just couldn't resist a squeeze of the fat, purple head. "See, getting harder by the second and good to go." Barlow rubbed himself against her thigh for good luck and turned to join the gathering at the fire pit.

Colton nodded a cursory hello to Barlow as he joined the circle around the roasting girl. Barlow nodded back, the vague look on his face letting Colton know he wasn't the only one here with a shit memory for names. Colton offered a half smile and pulled his dick out of his jeans. He held it in one hand and felt it harden in the heat from the fire.

As was customary in such gatherings, it was time to make the contribution. Colton, along with the other guys, began to masturbate. He always found it irritating—and somewhat rude—that some of the guys chose to continue their conversations about football, fishing, work, whatever; Colton preferred to remain silent and concentrate on the job in hand, pun intended.

David Green shot his load first. He came with a loud grunt and an entirely superfluous *"oh yeah!"* Colton knew from his nocturnal observations of the Greens that the poor guy *always* came too quickly. This was often evident by Patricia's disappointed face at the window on their sex nights. Green's semen sputtered onto Julie's golden, crisp body and sputtered and spat in the heat. Steam rose from the fresh cum, and Tom eased on the roast's rotation to keep as much on the meat as possible.

"Thank you, David, always appreciated," Tom said as he poked a fork into his daughter's side to check on the progress of her cooking. One had to wait until the juices ran clear before eating, and Julie's were still tinged with pink. Tom looked at his watch, all too aware as a good host that he was keeping hungry guests waiting.

Spent, his dick deflating, David backed away and headed off toward the cooler for more suds. His place at the ceremonial roast was taken by Leona Ashbrook.

Leona was a relative newcomer at the O'Keefe's parties. She had made her way onto the invitation hotlist because she had recently given birth to something that almost resembled a baby, although, rumor had it the thing was most likely amphibious in origin. Leona was a woman of average height with a thickset body and an unruly mop of the most brilliantly red hair. She had arrived at the party stripped to the waist for the occasion, and as she took over Green's place, she began to squeeze her engorged breasts and spray the roasting O'Keefe girl with her milk. As Leona kneaded and scrunched at her bloated tits, fine sprays of creamy milk shot out and splashed, hissing onto Julie's bubbling flesh. A few hair-thin streams went astray to spray the guys on either side of her with thin fountains of sticky milk. The guys seized this opportunity and repositioned themselves to catch the sprays on their dicks to jerk off in the warm, slippery fluid.

"Colton!" Tom called over the steaming, aromatic roast. "Try this." Tom wielded his carving knife with a connoisseur's ease and deftly sliced off one of Julia's perfectly cooked nipples. He held it out to Colton on the end of the glinting knife. Colton ceased his masturbating, took the nipple from the blade, and popped it into his mouth.

Colton chewed on the nipple; his taste buds delighted in just how tender and moist it was, and how the wonderful taste reminded him of the halcyon days of long summers and endless debauched delights with his beloved Alicia. Fighting back the tears, Colton swallowed the nipple down with an audible *gulp*. He nodded his approval at Tom, and a satisfied smile played on Colton's lips as he reached back down for his stiff cock.

"I think Barbara has other plans for that, buddy." Tom grinned as his wife reached around from behind Colton and took his penis in her hand.

"It would be my guess it's been a while since you fucked something other than that dog of yours." Barbara O'Keefe said in that low, sultry voice of hers. "Not since Alicia, eh?" She tugged gently on Colton's dick to lead him away from the group around the fire pit.

Colton shook his head. It felt strange to have another's hand around his dick, and strange had taken on a whole new meaning for Colton since the thing with Jethro, which apparently, the whole neighborhood knew about.

She led Colton out onto the back lawn; her naked ass wiggled provocatively as she walked and helped beyond help to maintain his tumescence. It was still raining, and the sickly, salty stink was all pervading and stuck to Colton's hair and face. As he admired the sensual curve of Barbara's spine and her full, round buttocks, he watched as the semen slid along Barbara's skin in pasty clumps. Barbara lay down on the soft grass; her body was wet with the semen rain, and she spread her legs far wider apart that Colton had thought possible to display the oozing, raw flesh of her vagina.

"So," she said as she looked up at him. "Fuck me."

And fuck her he did.

There was no need for Barbara to repeat her invitation; no, it was most definitely a *command*. Obediently, Colton shed his clothes and climbed aboard his neighbor's wife. And ah, she felt so fucking good inside. She was hot and wet, and he felt her cunt sucking at his penis head like a baby at a teat. Barbara pulled him deep inside her body with her honed vaginal muscles and buried her thumb deep into his clenched ass for good measure.

Colton pumped away at the delectable Mrs. O'Keefe. As he did so, he found that despite feeling more than a little self conscious, he was unable to prevent himself grunting as he revelled in the feel of a woman's pussy around his dick for the first time in far too long. He looked down at her firm, shimmering body as he fucked her, enjoying that slightly upturned face, half-closed eyes, and those formidable titties that bounced and jiggled atop her rib cage with each thrust like they were twin, wild creatures in a desperate bid for escape.

It wasn't too long before Colton could feel his orgasm building. It was disappointingly too soon for his liking, but it *had* been an extraordinarily long time between vaginas. Colton sensed his point of no return as it raced toward him like a galloping horse.

All of the sights, smells, and tastes of the party around him buoyed Colton along; the crisp, golden, roasting flesh of a well cooked young gal, the taste of her delectably barbecued nipple on his palate, the array of masturbating men around the flickering flames of the firepit, Joe Sonemaly slurping eagerly at the clergyman's engorged dick,

Honey-Lou Woolston's stretched, exposed vagina; this all served to drive Colton headlong toward the most explosive orgasm he could ever have imagined.

Colton felt the pressure draw his balls tight against his body and the head of his cock swell more than he thought physically possible inside the delightfully tight Mrs. O'Keefe. Colton knew, even if someone held a gun to his head right now, he wouldn't be able to stop the rhythm. And so, Colton Forshay came with such an explosive *"Ugh!"* it made his elbows tremble with such ferocity he feared he would collapse onto Barbara's semen and sweat-slicked body and crush her. The waves of the orgasm ripped through Colton's body like a lightening bolt, and he pumped stream after stream of cum deep into Barbara's cunt. There was so much of the pent-up stuff that he could feel it already beginning to squidge out of her against his dick, and he feared he would not stop ejaculating fluids until his body was a dried out, empty husk.

Another grunt, another spasm, and Colton came some more.

CHAPTER TWO

"Colton!" Zeenah's voice cut through his sleep like a shrill buzz saw. "For Christ's sake, wake up!"

Colton jolted himself awake. His eyes opened wide and immediately hurt in the harsh, morning light. Outside, he could hear the familiar mechanical *brrr* of another suburban Saturday morning as the lawn guys went about their business.

"Wassup?" he slurred as his mouth lagged behind the rest of his body in the waking up stakes. Colton leaned up on his elbows and turned his head to face his wife.

Zeenah sat up next to him in their bed. She had her back against the headboard, and her knees drawn up to her chest. She hugged her knees so tightly with lean, bronzed arms, that it looked like she was scared of something. Zeenah peered down at Colton with a disgusted look on her face that made him wonder if he'd shit in the bed.

Or something far, far worse even than that.

"I didn't?" he asked.

"You did," she said.

Colton studied his wife who looked as hot as ever in the black and red, silky nightgown he'd bought her for some anniversary or other back in the mists of time. This particular nightwear had always been a favorite with Colton; it was short and butt-skimming, and since Zeenah never wore panties to bed, there was always a chance of an accidental pussy flash. The gown was scooped low both at the front and under the arms and that combination always provided a goodly display of cleavage and bulging sideboob. Colton also admired the way the silk rode up his wife's smooth thighs to expose that tantalizing hint of ass cheek and plunged down to her pierced navel to allow her full breasts to bulge out. Colton wondered if his wife had even the slightest idea of what kind of effect the gown had on him. Perhaps if she did, she'd quit wearing it to bed.

And then he saw what he'd done.

"Oh shit," he sputtered. "I am *so* sorry, my love."

That's pretty much all he could think of to say, *all* there was to say since there was no denying his indiscretion. Colton stared at the incriminating evidence that glistened wetly on the hip of his wife's nightgown; the sticky, wet globs of semen seemed to twinkle and shine like misshapen pearls in the morning sunlight. He saw too, not without some pride, he had managed to splash some of the stuff up onto the side of one magnificent tit as well.

"You sleep-humped me, Colton." She had a knack these days of making anything sexual sound repulsive. "Again."

Zeenah was right, of course, there could be no denying it. And this was by no means the first time Colton had rubbed his dick to completion on his wife in bed—probably wouldn't be the last either. He looked down at the deflating tent between his own legs, which was where the cum had soaked through and was spreading into quite the formidable wet spot on the four-hundred count sheet.

Colton ventured a smile, a smile with a slight shrug of the shoulders in which he attempted to convey just how sorry he was, whilst at the same time, suggesting if she put out a little more at bedtime, this wouldn't be happening. Colton also smiled a private, inward smile at the fact that he'd obviously frottered Zeenah at the same time as he'd been dreaming about being balls-deep inside the incredibly wet and accommodating Mrs. O'Keefe.

"I think you should see someone." Zeenah ignored the smile that, at one time, would win her over no matter what may have transpired.

"Pardon me?" Colton was taken aback.

"You obviously have a problem, Colton," she said, her voice flat. "I think it would help you to talk to a—a professional." She attempted a smile of her own that, to Colton, came across as little more than a patronizing grimace.

"You can't be serious." Colton snorted. The only problem he could see here was his wife's lack of interest in his cock. Only, he couldn't really say that, could he?

"I've made you an appointment for this afternoon," Zeenah told him. "It's with Dr. Stackhouse. He really is very good."

This was a new name to Colton. As much as he racked his swirling brain, he couldn't place it anywhere.

"The who now?" was all he could manage as a reply.

"I've been seeing him for six months now." Zeenah further surprised her husband. "He's helped me a hell of a lot."

"With what?"

"With all of the changes that are happening in our marriage, Colton." Was that exasperation? "You know, since the kids left home."

Colton sank back into his pillow, nonplussed. He tried hard to think what could have possibly changed between he and Zeenah in the past year since the twins had gone off to college in California. And, as far as he could see, the only change had been the marked drop off in sexual activity. That, he had put down to her rapidly approaching menopause; after all, it had hit her mother at thirty-five. That gave Zeenah five years on her mom which he reckoned was good going, and he considered her libido declining before his—an inevitable consequence of marrying someone six years older than himself.

"Perhaps he can help you with your *sexsomnia*," Zeenah said with the same tone in her voice as when she saw an injured animal in the street or some severely disabled child struggling to do something for itself.

"Aw, come on, Zeenah, that's not even a real word," Colton protested. He was offended at the very idea but couldn't stop his eyes from wandering the length and breadth of his wife's firm body.

"It is so a real word, Colton. Dr. Stackhouse said so." Zeenah sounded petulant now and her lips pursed into the pout that made Colton want to slide his dick between them.

"If you say so, my love." Colton dampened the brewing argument with conciliation. The last thing he needed right now was a full-blown, blazing row with Zeenah. Not at the start of a rare weekend off and certainly not with the fresh stirring he was experiencing beneath the cotton sheet. As infuriating as she was being right now, Colton couldn't take his eyes off of Zeenah's semen-splashed nightgown, the expanse of smooth, tanned thigh, the sensuous swell of her full breasts, and that slightest hint of sparsely haired pink between her legs.

"Promise me you'll go see him, Colton," she said, her eyes searching his.

"I promise, sweetie." Colton reached for his wife's hand that still firmly gripped her knee. He shifted in the bed to face her, the bed sheet was glued to his penis with drying cum, and it moved with him.

"Really?!" Zeenah slapped his hand away and shuffled farther toward her own side of the bed. "That's all you can think about right now?"

Colton sighed and contemplated his wife; she was still stunningly beautiful after all these years and still drove him to distraction with that sensuous, firm body of hers. But what had become of the woman he loved who used to frequent sex clubs and orgies with him, and whose party trick was to take on nine dicks at once; one each in her cunt, ass, and mouth, one in each hand and foot, and one in each armpit? As Colton remembered with erotic delight, the drive home from such soirees had always been a treat, what with his wife looking like a wanton slut, all sticky and smelling of semen, and Colton with a dick so hard you could cut sheet rock with it—

Hold on a minute.

It was Alicia he was thinking about; the wife he had in his dreams; the woman he had dreamt he'd lost, who he struggled to remember in detail but could only recall the memory of her.

Colton decided right then that yes, perhaps he really ought to pay a visit to Dr. Stackhouse.

* * *

"Call me Zachary." The tall psychiatrist offered one hand for Colton to shake and ushered his new patient toward the comfy couch with the other. "Please, sit down."

Colton studied the man with wary eyes. Being of average height himself, he'd always been suspicious of the unusually tall, and Dr.—*call me Zachary*—Stackhouse was an easy six-three, six-four. He had a close-cropped haircut that seemed impossibly black, piercing blue eyes, and a broad mouth filled with what Colton presumed to be veneered teeth; no one grew their own teeth that straight and that white.

Colton sat down. His backside sank into the soft couch, and immediately, he felt at ease despite the towering shrink.

"I'm not sure why I'm here, really," Colton offered. "I mean, there's nothing wrong with me, *per se*." The latter, a favorite phrase of Colton's, drove Zeenah to distraction.

"Your wife is worried about you, Colton," Stackhouse said. "I *can* call you Colton, can't I?"

"Sure thing, Doc—I mean, Zachary," Colton replied. "What has she been saying about me?"

"I'm afraid I cannot discuss that. Doctor/patient confidentiality and all that." The tall man smiled and sat himself down in the chair opposite. Colton thought the shrink looked a little uncomfortable with his tall frame kind of folded up like that; the man's knees were almost level with his own chest.

"Seriously?" Colton mused over the fact the good doctor wasn't allowed by law to discuss what a wife divulged about her own husband to said husband. Sometimes this world seemed crazier than the dream world in which he'd gotten his own dog pregnant.

"This session is all about you, Colton." Stackhouse advised. "You can talk about whatever you like, anything that's on your mind. Even the weather if that's what takes your fancy." A broad smile.

The weather? What the fuck did Stackhouse think he was, British? And they both knew what ailed him; why he was here sitting on the world's comfiest couch with the world's tallest head doctor. And that was, quite simply, because Zeenah Forshay had deemed it necessary.

"I really don't know what to say," Colton said as his mind went a complete blank.

"You can say whatever is on your mind. It's totally your hour," Stackhouse said. "You don't actually have to say *anything* if you'd prefer a little silence. Some of my patients like to take this opportunity to enjoy some peace from their noisy lives. Some even take an hour's sleep." He made a light laughing sound at the back of his throat that sounded like a gargle.

Sleep. Now, there was a good idea. Colton figured he could do with some of that right now, although he was still reluctant at this stage to admit to himself the reason why.

He'd been rudely interrupted from the O'Keefe's party, and he had unfinished business.

Colton curled up on the sofa under the watchful eye of the shrink. He saw Stackhouse reach for a notepad and scribble away with a pen that looked like it cost more than Colton earned in three months. And then Colton's eyes closed, and he drifted off into a welcome sleep.

CHAPTER THREE

It was with some disappointment Colton found himself *not* at the O'Keefe's with the wondrous Barbara O'Keefe impaled on the end of his dick or that saliva-inducing aroma of barbecued human flesh, but at the Venegas' house instead. That meant it was Sunday already.

Colton struggled to regain his bearings and made his way into the living room where voices were raised, and raucous laughter resonated.

"Yo, Colton!" Aiden Venegas greeted him above the hubbub. "Look everybody, Colton's here!"

A loud cheer filled the room, and the happy crowd raised their cans of cheap, generic brand beer in Colton's honor. He recognized most of the faces from the O'Keefe's, including Tom and Barbara—the latter of the couple already stark naked and busy fingering her pussy on the shabby leatherette sofa. There were fewer people here than at the barbecue, as was always the case; this house was smaller, and Mrs. Venegas was not to everyone's taste. The Venegas' parties pared the neighborhood gang down to a select, hardcore few, of which Colton was obviously a member, albeit an absentee one for a couple of years. It felt heartwarming to be welcomed back into the fold with open arms—and legs—of course. As with the O'Keefe's barbecue, Colton hadn't planned to come right up until a last-minute change of heart. In the end, it had been Eric who had persuaded him to come. Actually, told him he really ought to get out more and circulate with the old crowd.

It had been a long, long time since Colton last attended one of Aiden and Elizabeth Venegas' BBW gatherings—that's Big Beautiful Woman to the uninitiated. He had begun to avoid them before Alicia's passing as both he and his wife were failing to see the attraction of the morbidly obese Elizabeth Venegas. The last party he could recall attending was way back when Elizabeth was a mere five-hundred pounds and could still walk—just barely.

"Hey, Aiden," Colton greeted his host. "Hey, Tom, George, Honey-Lou." He acknowledged those closest to him. Honey-Lou Woolston, as per, was attracting a large proportion of the attention as she had stapled her breasts together and was wearing a butt plug of epic proportions. The plug had a large, fake ruby at the end, which reflected light around the room and made for a kind of bizarre disco ball.

A can of chilled beer was thrust into Colton's hand. He stepped over a knee-high pile of bulging white trash bags and cracked open the beer. As he slurped down the cold, bitter-tasting liquid and looked at the squalor around him, Colton remembered exactly why he had begun to avoid the Venegas's parties in the first place.

It was not strictly fair to lay all of the blame for the Forshays' dwindling attendance on the fact that they found Aiden and Elizabeth to be cheap, crass, vulgar rednecks with all the social grace of chimpanzees. Colton and his late wife had actually had some good times there.

A large part of the reason for Colton and Alicia's persistent declining of the Venegas' invites was they had discovered the delights of a more exclusive sex club across town. The place was by invitation only—Alicia had been personally invited by one of the town councillors as she was sucking pickled cucumbers out of his asshole one evening in the park. Payment just to get in was anal sex (from both he *and* Alicia), a golden shower, and three used tampons. And, it had been more than worth that effort. The club had been an utter delight as the perversities, and the more discernible clientele on offer, had been eye opening even for the Forshays. Hell, the place even had its own stable, complete with freshly crucified stable girls and incredibly accommodating thoroughbred horses that were hung like—well—horses. All of which had served as a stark contrast to—this.

Colton looked around and found that very little had changed in his years of abstinence. Yep, the Venegas' home was pretty much as he remembered it.

Aiden and Elizabeth were hoarders and, as such, they threw very little—if anything—away. As a result, their home was crammed with trash that was mostly neatly contained within white, vanilla-scented trash bags that were twist-tied at the top. The trash bags were a result of Aiden's OCD, which made the whole thing almost seem quaint. Most of the rooms in their large house—Colton guesstimated it to be at least four thousand square feet, possibly five if you took into account the four-car garage with granny apartment—were filled to bursting with the trash bags. Many of the trash-filled rooms were impossible to get into, and there were one or two that had a labyrinth of tunnels through the mountains of trash bags, which could be fun to explore, providing you didn't mind the rats and the stench of leaking trash juice.

Aiden's stock reply as to the question *why* they threw nothing away had always been '*it might come in handy.*' As if years old pizza boxes, takeaway cartons, and used toilet paper would ever have a purpose sometime in the future. And it didn't go anywhere near to explaining why the toilets upstairs had never been flushed, and now they were blocked and overflowed a stinking, brown cascade of excrement down the staircase. It was no secret that Aiden now had to do his business in a bucket, and whilst his urine was stored in pop-top bottles in the pee fridge, heaven only knew where the crap wound up.

And yet, as was evident by the gathered neighbors, somehow the filthy conditions added to the overall eroticism of the gathering.

Elizabeth Venegas, of course, had no choice as to where she performed her toilets. She had grown so large of late that visiting the lavatory was no longer an option, and even if it hadn't been bunged up with God knows how many years' worth of shit, she'd have crushed the porcelain under her vast weight. As far as Colton knew, Elizabeth Venegas had exclusively occupied one of the only two truly habitable rooms in the house for at least two years now.

Of those rooms was the lounge, which, as expansive as it was, was beginning to show signs of the clutter of trash build-up. The white bags were stacked in small mounds in the corners, punctuated by piles of yellowing newspapers and out of date phone books. And then there was the playroom, which is where Elizabeth resided and where all the action happened. Colton found himself wandering toward the playroom, his sour, warming beer still in hand.

The playroom was completely devoid of trash. Not one of the otherwise ubiquitous white trash bags could be seen amongst the super-large bean bags that were scattered on the floor around Elizabeth Venegas. Colton guessed that might have something to do with Aiden's penchant for fattening his wife up to the point of immobility. The man had actually thrown a special party on the day Elizabeth declared she could no longer walk due to her bulk, and another when she reached eight-hundred pounds. No doubt there would be one real humdinger of a get-together when he got her to the magic one-thousand pounds he aspired to. Yep, Aiden Venegas was just your typical feeder, who got his kicks out of making his wife as fat as humanly possible, and then some. Colton figured it was all part of the same quirky psychological short circuit that compelled Venegas to store his trash in vanilla-scented bags and keep them in the house. The feeding of Elizabeth was just another aspect of the hoarding behaviour. You feed food into Elizabeth's cavernous mouth, and there it stayed in the form of those copious rolls of flab; hence, no need for trash in the playroom.

"Colton Forshay, as I live and breathe!" Elizabeth's deep, husky voice reached him through the grunts and moans of the playful people in the room. "Take out that dick and come let Mama Venegas take a good look at ya!"

Colton slipped his penis from his pants—he'd had enough foresight to go commando today—and made his way toward the pink mountain of a woman that sat in the middle of the room.

"Hey, Colton," Joe Sonemaly grunted as Colton made his way between two naked guys he'd never seen before.

"Hey, Joe," Colton replied. "David, Patricia." He greeted the Greens as he got within literal spitting distance of Elizabeth.

Patricia Green grunted what appeared to be a muffled *hello* to Colton. From what Colton could see of her, he could tell that she was naked. Her head and most of her upper torso were buried beneath an avalanche of Elizabeth's voluminous belly folds, and from the sound of it, she was busy lapping away at the obese woman's clit. David Green smiled down at his wife's raised ass from his position behind Elizabeth; his dick was nestled snugly in a fat fold on the fat woman's back.

Another couple of guys—one of whom Colton recognized as Cameron Flynn—busied themselves rubbing their engorged members on parts of Elizabeth's skin on the undersides of her arms that had toughened over the years into something that resembled elephant hide, and a young black guy was merrily dipping his glans into an open sore on her thigh. Colton took it all in; *different strokes and all that*, he thought to himself.

Margaret Flynn, clad in a toe-to-neck silver latex catsuit sat astride one of Elizabeth's impossibly wide legs. Her own thighs gripped around the pale, dough-flesh that covered down to the woman's corpulent ankles. Margaret appeared in her own private ecstasy as she rubbed her crotch on the big woman's foot and sucked on a pair of hard cocks that had been presented to her; only one of which was still attached to its owner. The other, still erect despite losing copious amounts of blood that splashed over Margaret's latex-covered tits, protruded from her mouth and looked like some sick, exploding, trick cigar. Unable to talk—obviously—Margaret waved her hello to Colton and patted the head of the newly dickless guy who was drinking Margaret's fragrant sweat that had accumulated in the catsuit from a small hole he had nicked in one of the toes.

Elizabeth Venegas reached out and took Colton firmly by the dick.

"It's been a long time, Colton." She smiled as she massaged him to tumescence with expert, chubby fingers.

"Yes, it has, Elizabeth." Colton acknowledged as Elizabeth fondled him. "How have you been?"

Of course, Colton could see how she had been for himself. Since the last time he'd had the pleasure, Elizabeth had ballooned to well over eight-hundred pounds, and her face had swelled with adipose tissue to the point where her eyes were little more than squinting slits in a wobbling sea of pale, pudgy flesh. Her arms were now thicker than Colton's thighs, whilst her own thighs thicker than his trunk; and her trunk—well, that was buried beneath roll upon roll of blubber that shook and undulated as the men around her used her body to take their pleasure.

Elizabeth was naked, of course; Colton doubted if anyone actually made clothing for her size—she had gone beyond XXXXXL some time ago, and was pretty much "welcome to the circus" size. And, even if they did make clothes her size, Aiden, the party guests, and Elizabeth's followers on her popular webcam show preferred the Magnificent Mrs. Venegas in all of her nude glory. She sat in the center of the playroom, propped up by huge beanbags. Her monstrous breasts lolled down her front and rested their bulk upon her gargantuan stomach. The nipples on both breasts were stretched and distorted and resembled dusky, pink versions of relief maps of some obscure, former Soviet-bloc country; one that invariably ended in _stan_.

"Ya want me to suck on this a while, sugar?" Elizabeth purred with a glint in her eye. Colton glanced down at the guy who was merrily sucking on Margaret Flynn's foot sweat. The bloodied mess of the guy's crotch and the way his skin was paling due to blood loss dampened Colton's ardour somewhat.

"Thank you, but no, Elizabeth," he said. "This is just fine." He glanced down at his penis, which was all but smothered by the fat woman's hand. Last thing he wanted was his dick anywhere near the glutton's mouth.

"Ya want to stick it in me, then?" Elizabeth persisted.

Colton briefly contemplated the offer, as romantic as it was. His mind spun back to the first time he'd been presented with the humongous Mrs. Venegas for the purposes of sexual congress. He'd asked Aiden how one was supposed to have sex with such a formidable woman.

"S'easy, son. Ya just pick a fold that ain't got fungus growing in it."

To the point, as was Aiden's style. Although, it wasn't so much the fungus that spawned and multiplied in the myriad creases and trenches of Elizabeth's obesity—if anything, Colton had discovered that could heighten the sensation and was not a problem providing he washed in hot water following sex—it was the stink of stale cum some of the deeper crevasses harbored that he found could be the most off-putting. And that was in the time when Aiden would roll his wife out onto the front lawn and rinse her down with a garden hose. Even then he didn't always get all of it; some of his wife's fat was virtually impenetrable, by hose or even the most probing of cocks. Nowadays, Colton had been told, Aiden rarely rinsed her down as she had gotten too big for him to maneuver, even through the especially widened doorways he'd made in the house. Now, she just stank of rancid sweat and stale semen, and a guy just had to take potluck where he fucked her.

Elizabeth tugged on Colton's dick, indicating he should penetrate a particularly juicy crinkle of fatty skin adjacent to her armpit. She hocked and spat onto the head of his prick and slid it in.

Colton was forced to admit to himself that yes, it felt mighty good, and yes, he had missed it.

"How goes it, Colton, old friend?" David Green said with a cheery tone.

"Pretty good, thanks," Colton replied. He waved at George McLaughlin and the Reverend Smallwood as they entered the room, dicks flopping on a semi-hard, and eager to savor the formidable delights that were Elizabeth Venegas.

"Nice to see you out and about. Everyone's missed you," David persisted.

"It's good to be out," Colton replied, his breath coming out a little short as he thrust into Elizabeth's fat. "I know; it's been far too long."

"It has that." David smiled. He reached over and gave his wife's ass a mighty slap that left a glowing red handprint on her left buttock. "Patricia and I were only saying the other day how much we missed you and Alicia." No glimmer of apology in his eyes there. "Especially the way she used to eat out Patricia's pussy. Quite the skilled tongue, your good lady wife, by all accounts." He slapped Colton on the shoulder.

Colton managed a smile. There it was. The Greens figured he should be over Alicia by now and, by association, Colton figured so did everyone else. He and Alicia had been great friends with David and Patricia, and to Colton's recollection, Alicia hadn't been the only one with an expert tongue. He'd spent many a happy evening with David's dick in his ass watching Patricia and Alicia sixty-nine for their entertainment, and then he'd fucked Patricia and kissed her deep while her face was still sticky with his wife's pussy juice.

"So," David said, his face flushed as he neared orgasm. "How *have* you been?"

"Okay, I guess," Colton replied. "Keeping myself busy with keeping the house in one piece and taking care of Eric."

"You managing okay for credits?" David asked, as direct as ever. "Because, if you're struggling—"

"I'm fine, honestly." Colton was embarrassed. Financial discussions always made him feel uncomfortable, and he certainly didn't want to look like a charity case to David Green. The truth was, although he had quit work after Alicia's death, Colton had barely scratched the surface of the TV show's compensation. They'd given him double the usual rate with some bullshit story about how her demise had been voted best in season.

"That's good to know, old boy." David slapped Colton's shoulder again.

"Yep, and as long as this works." He pointed to his dick that was buried in Elizabeth's blubber. "I won't be needing money."

David Green quit his thrusting and grabbed Colton's arm.

"Money?" he whispered. "Did you just say *money*?"

"Er—no, what I meant was—" Colton stammered, at once realizing his mistake.

Money didn't exist in this dream world.

"I know what you meant, Colton." David looked at him concerned. Elizabeth looked up at them both with a quizzical look in her squinty eyes. David recommenced this thrusting, and Colton followed suit, even though his desire had diminished somewhat, along with some of his erection. "You mean where you pay for things with little metal discs and bits of fancy paper instead of dick, pussy, ass and mouth." David lowered his voice still further. "You've had the dream too?"

Colton nodded. Of course, the absurdity of the situation was not lost on him; the people in his dream world were persecuted for dreaming snippets of the real world which he guessed were simply machinations of his own mind. As much of a mind-fuck as that was to get his head around, it made for nice, escapist dreams. So, Colton decided to roll with it, not wanting to break the spell here. And besides, Elizabeth Venegas's arm fat sure did feel good, despite the acrid smell that assaulted his nose every time she moved.

"I know you've been out of circulation a while, but even you must know that talk like that can get you taken away." David sounded concerned. "President Ocelot has been clamping down hard on the Dreamers recently, surely you've heard?"

Colton had heard, or to be more precise, he *knew*.

President Ocelot, who was actually an ocelot (as in the Texas big cat) who had the power of telepathic mind control, had in recent years been hunting down citizens who dared to even mention dreaming about the other world. No one knew for sure why, only that those who were taken in by the President's dream squads were never seen or heard of again.

"You need to keep it to yourself, David," Colton said as his thrusts into Elizabeth quickened.

"You too, buddy," David said. "Neither of us would want that getting out, now would we?" David's thrusts into Elizabeth's back fold increased, his breath coming in short bursts. "Tell me, you don't dream about the single storey house with the white-painted flashing and the—"

"White picket fence?" Colton finished the sentence for David, who was distracted and ejaculating deep into Elizabeth's fatty crevasse. "And the apple tree, and the gingham curtains." He added with a smile and a grunt as he pulled back and shot his load over Elizabeth's flabby arm.

Both men laughed as they came together.

"You got it, Colton. Schtum's the word," David panted, his face flushed with his exertions.

"How was that, Colton my dear?" Elizabeth enquired as she lapped at Colton's spillage on her inflated upper arm. "Colton? Colton?" She insisted, and her voice lowered, and she sounded to Colton almost exactly like—

***

"Colton?" Dr. Stackhouse shook his patient gently. "I'm afraid that's all the time we have for today."

Colton awoke to the expanse of the shrink's face over his, all else obscured. He struggled awake, the stink of

Elizabeth Venegas stinging his nostrils. The feel of her liquid flesh on his cock stayed with him, along with the warm, wet stickiness of ejaculate in his pants.

"Oh, er, I am so sorry—" he sputtered. "I didn't mean to—"

"It's okay, Colton, nothing to get upset about." Stackhouse glanced down at the obvious, if somewhat diminishing erection and widening wet spot on his patient's trousers and suppressed a smile. "It would seem that we have plenty to talk about at our next meeting."

CHAPTER FOUR

It was late Friday afternoon, and Colton was still at work, much to his chagrin. The Dead Shift, they called it here at the illustrious offices of Barnett, Schuster, and Wolfe; the thirteenth largest accountancy firm in town (or the *fourth smallest*, depending upon which way you preferred to look at such things). Friday afternoons on the fifth floor—Bookkeeping—were always dull affairs. Not just because the work was, at best, tedious, but because even though Mr. Christian (he insisted on being called that, Colton guessed he was a frustrated schoolmaster), the department manager always left straight after lunch, and everyone else just kept right on working until five-thirty.

Colton stared at the spreadsheet displayed on his computer screen. His heart not in it, his brain struggled to register the numbers that populated the little boxes under the twelve-point, bold headings. Even to Colton's trained eye, the numbers today were just a uniform array of straight lines and a surreal pattern that looked to him like the coat of some exotic big cat.

An Ocelot, perhaps?

A species peculiar and indigenous to Texas. A creature rarely seen and on the endangered list, the Ocelot, whilst hardly in the same league as lions and tigers, was a beautiful looking animal and considerably bigger than your average domestic tabby.

And, of course, it was also the president of Colton's bizarre dream world. Although, for the life of him, he couldn't fathom why his brain had plucked that particular creature out of his imagination.

Colton had not dreamt of the dream place since the Venegas' party dream, quite possibly because of the disgrace he'd made of himself in Stackhouse's office. Following that particular episode of abject shame, he had thought long and hard—pun pardoned—about what Zeenah now referred to as his "problem" and had come to pretty much the same conclusion.

Whilst Colton had always been dissociative when it came to sex, he likened sexual release to any other of the body's necessary functions—much like taking a dump. He had discovered, of late, his desire for sex had increased considerably. Perhaps of deeper concern was he found his desire was inversely proportional to Zeenah's willingness to let him fuck her. Perhaps then, Colton considered, this was why he'd not paid a visit to his dream world in almost a week. Zeenah had been relatively okay with him since his trip to the shrink, sympathetic even, and she'd allowed him to make love to her on two occasions since then. She still referred to sex as *conjugals,* though, which took away a little of the frisson for Colton. And her "pull my nightie down when you've finished" pet phrase could be off-putting at times; but all things considered, it did feel good to slip into her hot, wet vagina again.

Almost as good as Alicia's.

But then, toward the end of the week, his wife had gone back to being a cold bitch again.

Colton felt tired. He'd not slept for shit this week, what with the unexpected *conjugals* with Zeenah, and her subsequent cold shoulder in bed—who knew his wife could cling so precariously to her edge of the bed and not fall off? Sleep had been erratic and hard to come by. He peeked out from his cubicle and saw there was no one around. With Christian gone and lunchtime over, no one would be venturing out of their own little five-by-five world until home time, with the possible exception of Chuck Pope from Sales Ledger who had a bladder the size of a walnut.

Colton rested his head on his desk and closed his eyes. He figured that if anyone asked, he'd just say he was taking a power nap. Wasn't that what all the executives on the top floor did? Hell, they even had a custom-built power nap *room* up there complete with memory-foam mattresses, the lazy bastards.

***

Rape was on the TV again. There was a late seventies/early eighties broad getting double teamed by the show's house rapists, and she was kicking up as much of a fuss as she could muster given her advanced years. The show was no longer the favorite it once was in the Forshay household, but Colton would still tune in every now and then, despite what had happened to Alicia. However, when they had the oldies on, it always bored him. For a start, they were never all that pleasant to look at with their wrinkled, liver spotted skin, tragically sagging tits and lifeless, flappy genitals. And then there was the fact that they never lasted as long as the younger contestants, unable to put up even half the fight as their younger counterparts. Colton half suspected this was because they might actually enjoy the fact they were getting some sex, no matter in what circumstances; might as well enjoy it and go out with a bang, right?

"Well, this is boring," Eric piped up. "You can see she's not going to make it to the commercial break. See, she's already bleeding from her ass." He waved a paw toward the TV set where, sure enough, a dark froth of blood was bubbling from the old lady's anus as the huge guy with the wrist-thick dick pumped away at her.

Eric shuffled on the couch in an attempt to get comfortable, and his long tail lolled over the side. He was an odd-looking creature, which was to be expected from a boxer/shepherd/Colton mix. Eric was long, almost seven feet nose to tail tip and weighed in at a hundred and fifty pounds. He sported a luxurious brindle coat that shimmered in sunlight and long, thickset legs, each of which ended with a massive paw. Eric's head was almost that of a human; he had a not unattractive human face, oversized, floppy ears, and an elongated snout. His snout, which was peppered with greying hairs, protruded from his flat face and had canines that were a little more prominent than one would expect had he been totally human.

His mom—or father, as it happened to be, biologically speaking—had vamoosed pretty much the minute Eric was out of her *(him?)* and had only just taken the time to make the lame excuse to Colton that he *(she?)* needed space to find him/herself. So, Colton had been both mom and dad to young Eric and had raised him to have the best aspects of both species (by the time he was two, Eric could read, write, and fetch sticks.) The two had grown to truly enjoy each other's company. On his more reflective occasions, Colton would look at his son/dog and think just how much Alicia would have loved him.

Eric and Colton got along famously living as they did; the life of two bachelors in the large house. Eric could carry a great conversation and always kept himself abreast of current affairs with the daily newspapers. So, there was always something to spark a lively, intelligent exchange. And to Colton's relief, Eric had a keen instinct for when his dad/master wished to be left alone with his thoughts.

Colton sank into the couch taking care not to squash Eric's back paws that were spreading over onto his cushion. He allowed his mind to wander away from the dull gameshow that was close to reaching its inevitable conclusion; the old girl had all but stopped screaming now.

He found himself feeling weary; there'd been a hellish line at the grocery store that afternoon, which had added an hour to Colton's already overlong trip to pick up the week's provisions. There'd been some old boy having trouble keeping his dick hard to pay for his meagre basket of tinned goods, most of which appeared to be for a cat.

Colton had, rather unfortunately, an accidental ringside seat to the whole depressing spectacle, as he was next in line. The old man had been standing there, pants around his ankles, droopy dick in hand, grinding it between his thumb and forefinger with increasing desperation, like he was trying to squeeze some semblance of life into the poor old thing. Seeing this pathetic plight, his checkout girl—an attractive twenty something with a pair of the perkiest breasts Colton had seen in a long time—beckoned over the hot, Asian checkout girl one register over, and the two began making out in front of the old man.

Not a twitch, although the glint in the old man's eye was something to behold as he watched the checkout girls French kiss and pull at each other's clothes. But still, nothing in his nether regions, and he was beginning to look a little panicked. Colton figured the old man—easily in his eighties—had either hit his past-due date or had overspent in another store that morning.

Before long, the checkout girls were naked; their pert titties pressed tightly together, fingers dipping in and out of wet pussies like there was just no tomorrow. They maneuvered their lithe bodies onto the conveyor, pushing aside the old man's tins with perfectly manicured toes, and took up a *soixante-neuf*, with heads buried between each other's thighs. There, they'd slurped noisily at each other's glistening wet vaginas like kids with ice cream cones.

And still the old boy twiddled with his withered cock, his face a mask of utter panic as he stared down at the lifeless thing in his hand, even as checkout gal number one came. She screamed out, although her voice was muffled by her girlfriend's labia. She bucked and yelled out obscenities in her ecstasy, almost throwing the other girl off both herself and the conveyor. The Asian girl dug her fingers into the firm thighs that gripped her head, buried her tongue deep into the vagina that tightened around it almost to the point of pushing it out again. And then it was her turn for release, which she did with a little more reserve than her counterpart. A most feminine grunt and a sighed "Ohhh," and she relaxed her body to rest on top of her colleague.

The small crowd that had gathered to enjoy the spectacle had clapped politely and smiled their approval, all with the exception of the old man who had given up on his dick and was pulling up his pants.

"Freeze!" a booming voice made everyone jump.

Colton looked around and saw a pair of uniformed cops race into the grocery store, guns pulled and aimed squarely at the poor old man.

The shoppers who had gathered to enjoy the Sapphic show began to discretely disperse; the Asian checkout girl climbed off of her playmate and sidled back to her own register, still gloriously naked, her face glinted wet and slick from her endeavours at the other girl's juicy cunt.

The old man stood, pants half pulled up, like a rabbit frozen in oncoming headlights. Colton watched the man's eyes twitch as he weighed his options, as limited as they appeared to be right now. He could see the red light spots from the cop's guns as they danced on his face, and Colton realized at that moment, if he could see the old man's eye movements, then he was far too close for comfort. The cops here were not known for their good marksmanship.

Colton began to back away as the cops closed in, and his checkout girl clambered off the conveyor. She picked up her uniform and crouched down behind the register with a fearful expression on her lipstick-smeared face.

"There's no need to be hasty," the old man implored. "I'll come back later. You know, when things are working again." He waggled his shrinking dick about a little and attempted a smile at the stone-faced cops. To Colton, it had looked like less of a smile and more like the old man was throwing up in his mouth a little.

"You are under arrest for failure to pay," the older of the two cops informed the old man. "You will come with us." He grabbed at the handcuffs on his belt with expert ease, held them out to the old man.

"This is just a silly misunderstanding, there really is no—" The old man turned and ran, still holding his pants up with one hand.

Colton had winced at that point, knowing damn well what a serious mistake the poor old guy had just made. Perhaps he had known his time was up, that he would never be able to pay for groceries again, and he'd be disposed of anyway? It was common knowledge—although only spoken about in hushed tones and in private—once you could no longer pay your dues, you were simply taken away by the police to be removed from society. Permanently.

Old Boy had made it as far as the deli counter, which was much father than Colton figured he'd get, but most probably because the cops had fancied a little sport to break up an otherwise mundane day.

The old man's head popped open as the first bullet hit his skull. Blood, brain matter, and teeth peppered the glass-fronted counter and obscured the delicious array of sliced cold cuts on display. Before the old man hit the floor, another two bullets exploded his head into myriad fragments of jellied brain and skull bone onto which clung the old man's old, wiry, white hair. He'd hit the floor with a soggy *thwack*, let out a loud fart, and then he had lay there quite still as blood pumped from the remnants of his head, which was pretty much nonexistent from the lower jaw upward.

"Clean up on aisle four," a tinny voice had boomed through the P.A. system.

Colton sighed. He could have well done without seeing that today. He was down enough as it was without being reminded that one day, that could easily be him; a penis doesn't stay working forever. He returned his attention to the TV. A new episode of *Rape* was coming on, along with its jolly title sequence of happy, smiling contestants and theme tune that you just couldn't help but hum along to.

A feeling of dread settled in Colton's stomach, a tingling in his scalp. It was a rerun of Alicia's episode. And there she was, his beautiful wife on contestants' row, all smiles and wonderfully naked; her bare breasts jiggling as she waved like a crazy person into the camera. Of course, the podiums behind where the contestants stood were made of glass, so the studio audience and the viewers at home wouldn't miss out on seeing the three nude contestants in all their glory; Colton could clearly make out his Alicia's sensual, pouting labia.

"You want me to turn this off, Colton?" Eric asked, in command of the remote as usual. "There's the Interstate Scissoring Championships channel forty-two."

Colton shook his head. This was the first time he'd seen her episode since its live recording two years ago. He had managed to avoid its many reruns until now. When it was recorded, he had been in the audience along with the proud husbands of the other contestants—front row—to witness first-hand Alicia's moment of glory.

It was considered an honor of the highest degree to be chosen for the show, even more so to have one's wife chosen. Only the most beautiful, sexually adventurous women were selected; the very best of the best in each of the categories; and Alicia's category—the under thirty's—was notoriously difficult to get into. But, somehow, that thought didn't diminish Colton's feeling of loss or the fact that he missed his wife terribly. Also, the sex credits he'd been awarded by the show's production company didn't take away the pain of losing the one person in his life who had been so perfectly in tune with him.

"It's okay, Eric," Colton said. "I guess I have to face this sometime or other." It was not as if any of the show would come as a surprise to Colton. Not only had he actually been there in the audience at the time, but he had replayed it step by step, every detail over and over in his mind, over the past twenty-four months. Nope, there was nothing new coming up, and perhaps this was part of his process in coming to terms with losing Alicia.

The camera panned across each of the three contestant's faces, followed by a slow pan down to show off their exposed bodies. And then the host, a bizarre looking man by the name of Jeff Jefferson, bounced onto the stage to announce the qualifying round of the game. Jefferson was a diminutive man, no more than three feet in height with a dark, leathery perma-tan and a shiny silver suit. He always gripped his microphone too tight and spoke in a high, squeaky voice that could quite hurt the ears whenever he got over excited, which seemed to be a lot during the course of each episode.

The first round of the show—*fastest fingers first*—was quite simply the lady who could masturbate herself to orgasm the quickest. Each of the women had a small, round sensor taped to their head which monitored brain waves and serotonin levels to ensure no cheating, and off they went. The studio audience were encouraged (by means of large placards, Colton remembered) to cheer on and motivate as the three contestants frantically rubbed at their clitorises behind the glass podiums in their attempt to climax ahead of each other. Alicia came with a scream and at lightning speed within forty seconds—a show record—and stood gripping her podium for support, panting and waiting for the other two ladies to finish up. That was a worthwhile wait, for the audience at least, since contestant number three turned out to be a gusher, and she created a formidable puddle between her feet when she came to rapturous applause and a spot prize of a kitchen makeover.

Jeff Jefferson beckoned Alicia to center stage and patted her bare behind as she stood next to him. Jefferson was standing on a silver box that made him the same height as Alicia, although the camera angle was such that you couldn't see it on the TV. There was a cut to the audience, and Colton saw his own face smiling stupidly at his nude wife.

"Welcome, contestant number one, Alicia Forshay!" Jeff Jefferson said, his irritating voice raised at least an octave as he spoke.

Any higher, Colton thought, *and only Eric would be able to hear him.*

"Not only do you win the first round, but you get a thousand extra bonus points for being the fastest fingers—ever!" The audience went wild.

"And now, folks," Jefferson hushed the audience with his sincerest, serious voice. "It's time for Alicia to play the Big Prize round." The audience applauded yet again, and Colton noted a handful of *whoops* he didn't recall from the live show.

He thought Alicia had never looked so beautiful. She stood on that stage, tall and majestic, tanned breasts firm and heaving, her whole body glinting with a light sheen of orgasmic afterglow. And there was her smile, that broad, beaming smile that so complemented her shining eyes it made Colton ache inside.

The curtain went up and the Big Prize round commenced. The rules of the game were perfectly simple; the contestant had to prevent the show's resident rapists from entering them to the point of ejaculation—vagina or anus only, the mouth was deemed too easy—at all cost. As for the rapists, their job was to gain entry to the contestants by any means possible. The longer a contestant lasted without succumbing to their assailant, the more points, and the more points, the bigger the prize.

Alicia, as with all contestants selected for the show, had been asked to sign a disclaimer that abdicated all and any responsibility to the show's producers should she be injured or killed. And since deaths were commonplace due to the often-brutal enthusiasm of both rapists and contestants, the disclaimer doubled as a Transfer of Winnings document to allow next of kin to claim the prize credits.

Clever, that.

Colton remembered, with startling clarity, the guy who was pitted against Alicia that night. A giant of a man, as broad as he was tall—an easy six feet—buck naked, and with the longest, thickest dick Colton had ever seen. It looked, to Colton, like a third leg that had been chopped off at the knee. As Colton watched the huge man-mountain stride by on his TV screen, he recalled the sick ball that had settled in the pit of his guts during the recording at the realization of what was about to happen. That and the cloying scent of the man's body odor as it wafted by. Thankfully, that was something the TV didn't have to offer.

Whilst he'd seen Alicia fuck other men before—they were certainly no strangers to the swinging scene—this was different in so many ways, not least the fact that Colton now knew the conclusion to this particular scenario. And so, with tragic irony, Colton forced himself to watch the show on the sixty-eight-inch plasma screen he'd bought with the credits his wife had won on the show.

At first, Alicia put up one hell of a fight. She kicked and punched and scratched at the man, and there were times it looked like the big guy was about to give up, but then he fought back. He grabbed at Alicia's tits like they were Play-Doh, and squeezed them until they turned blue and she yelped in pain. He bit at her nipples and forced his fat, meaty fingers up inside her cunt until she cried, but to her credit, she still wasn't letting that monster cock anywhere near either of her precious orifices.

Absently, Colton found himself rooting for Alicia, as if, somehow, he could will the outcome to be different. The colossal man had Alicia pinned down now, and Colton knew this was the point at which his wife was tiring. The rapist had been prodding away at her with his impossibly hard penis for almost twenty minutes, and although his victim had visibly hurt him several times, there seemed to be no let up in his stamina. He straddled Alicia and trapped her arms by her sides with his muscular thighs. He reached behind himself and tried to prize her legs apart, but she was having none of that. Alicia bucked and struggled and screamed and spat, much to the delight of Jeff Jefferson who had, by then, whipped himself up into a barely audible frenzy.

Alicia's assailant shifted his bulk and knelt beside her. He pulled her up off the floor by her breasts and slammed her back down again. Her head hit the hard studio floor with a dull *thud,* and her body slackened just a little. The rapist seized his chance and thrust a powerful hand between Alicia's legs and grabbed her pussy hard. She screamed out in agony and grabbed at his arm in an attempt to sit herself up. He pushed her back down and pulled his hand from her cunt, making a big show of how dry his fingers remained.

Colton could remember thinking at the time, what a perfect defence; let's see the big bastard get his massive cock into her bone-fucking-dry.

The big guy thumped Alicia in the face, square on the nose. Her head smacked back onto the floor again, and her nose erupted in a fountain of scarlet. Grinning broadly, the rapist scooped a handful of the freely flowing blood and smeared it onto his dick. And with that, he pulled the dazed Alicia's thighs wide apart, positioned himself, and thrust deep into her gaping vagina.

And, as Colton watched helplessly, somewhere between struggling to fight against the blood that drained down her throat, arching her back to throw off the hefty assailant whose bulk was crushing her, and the agony of being forcibly entered by such a monster dick, Alicia's eyes glazed over, and she died.

The show's adjudicators then argued amongst themselves as to whether or not she had died before or after he had emptied his balls into her, which made a difference in the prize awarded, apparently. Finally, they settled on the conclusion that she had died *before* the ejaculation which meant she had indeed earned the Big Prize.

That is to say, Colton had.

The part they don't give away when the show runs on the TV is the hour or so it takes to clean up. After the three to four hours it takes to film the one-hour show, there was the blood and copious amounts of bodily fluids to mop up from the studio floor, bodies to dispose of, spent assailants to usher away. And all the while, the studio audience sat patiently and listened to the warm-up guy, who as far as Colton could recall, wasn't all that funny.

On the televised rerun, all they got were the commercials to cover the edits between segments; each time the show returned, the stage was pristine, and another naked contender stood on Contestant's Row. Colton tuned out the asinine commercials and tried to push the show to the back of his mind. Yes, he knew every part of his wife's part on the show by heart, but actually *seeing* it again, it seemed somehow rawer and more brutal than he remembered it, more *real*.

But, for all of that, he had got to see his beautiful Alicia again, and a part of him wished he'd set the DVR.

Colton's front door smashed inward and splinters of fractured wood and shards of glass showered into the living room. Startled into inactivity, Colton just turned his head and stared blankly at the two Dream Enforcement Officers who had just burst into his home. Eric, on the other hand, leaped from his chair and ran at the cops, teeth bared, and his throat making that odd growling noise that sounded more like a sixty-a-day octogenarian clearing phlegm from her larynx than a dog. It crossed Colton's adrenaline-soaked brain to call after his dog/son to prevent him from doing anything stupid, but Eric's canine instinct had obviously overruled his human sensibilities, and he was going for the kill.

With nonchalance, one of the DEO guys tasered Eric without so much as breaking a sweat, and Eric hit the floor twitching and spur pee all over the living room rug.

"DEO!" the other guy, resplendent in his charcoal gray uniform, shouted at Colton. A somewhat superfluous statement, since he had those exact letters emblazoned on his chest, and across his back. "On your fucking knees!" he commanded.

Colton was still in shock, his mind reeling. He desperately tried to think who in God's name could have reported him to the DEO, since he'd only ever mentioned his dreams to Eric, who he trusted implicitly.

"Money? Did you just say money?"

Shit, there had been his inadvertent slip in front of David Green. Surely not David, though? They'd fucked Elizabeth Venegas's fat together, so no way he'd report Colton for a slip of the tongue. Or perhaps it had been Elizabeth Venegas herself, who he'd assumed wouldn't pay attention to any of the conversations going on between the men and women that used her gargantuan body for their own debauched pleasures.

Yes, it had to have been her, the fat snitch. Not that any of it mattered to Colton right now; not when he was facing DEOs in his own home. Colton slid off the couch and knelt as requested. Instinctively, he placed his hands on the top of his head, fingers laced, as he'd seen in a thousand TV cop shows.

"Colton Forshay, you are under arrest for illegal dreaming—"

"There must be some mistake," Colton stuttered. "I have never—"

Colton's words were cut off as he felt a sharp prick in his neck and the vicious jolt of the DEO cop's taser. He lost all control of his muscles and dropped to the floor in an untidy heap, his arms and legs twitching and flailing uncontrollably. Colton's vision blurred, and his hearing sank beneath the intolerable buzzing inside his head.

Mercifully, before his bowels and bladder gave out, Colton slipped away from consciousness.

***

"Are you sure you're okay, Colton?" a voice as unexpected and jolting as the taser's sting brought Colton back with a start. He turned his head and saw Zeenah staring at him with a look of concern on her face. He also took note that she was looking particularly hot this fine evening, and he began to subconsciously gauge his chances of seduction.

"You've been quiet ever since you got home," she said.

Colton took stock of his surroundings. He was no longer at his home with Eric, nor at the office where he'd fallen asleep at his desk.

This meant he'd somehow made it home whilst still technically asleep, a twenty-five-minute drive through rush hour traffic and all.

"I-I'm fine," Colton assured his wife. Not sure how his somnambulant trip home had been at all possible, Colton switched his attention to his nether region to make sure his electrically stimulated accident hadn't followed him from the dream.

Thankfully, it had not.

The phone rang, which made Colton jump and almost caused the aforementioned urine-based accident. He picked up, and it was Mr. Christian—who never, ever called Colton at home, especially at six on a Friday evening.

"Colton. I'm calling to ask that you make yourself available for a meeting at a quarter after ten on Tuesday morning." Mr. Christian's booming voice echoed out from Colton's cell phone. A chill ran up his spine. This didn't sound good, "make yourself available" was never a good phrase to hear, let alone on a Friday evening. What the fuck had he done to warrant this? "And you can take Monday off,"

Mr. Christian continued as matter of fact and emotionless as usual. "Have a nice weekend, Colton."

And with that, Colton's boss hung up on him.

"What was that about?" Zeenah quizzed.

"I really have no idea, my love," Colton replied. He had a reasonably good idea, generally speaking, but was being truthful with her about the specifics. Today wasn't the first time he'd fallen asleep at his workstation, although it was the first time he'd not actually remembered waking up or getting home. *Just what the hell had he done in between times?*

"Well, I hope you're not being let go again." Zeenah hissed. "I've just put down a deposit on a new convertible."

Aha, so that was why she had gone out that morning wearing that short, low cut dress and five-inch, fuck-me heels. Zeenah knew from experience there was nothing to beat dressing like a wanton slut when it came to negotiating a deal with a salesman.

"I'm sure it's nothing to worry about, my love." Colton patted her knee, daring to slide his hand a little along her smooth, bare leg. Zeenah slapped her husband's hand away and launched herself from the sofa as if she'd been bitten on the ass. Then, to add insult to injury, she threw him a look that would have withered even the hardiest of constitutions, and for the first time outside of his dream world, Colton really missed Alicia.

CHAPTER FIVE

Colton spent the next day working out in the yard. He'd decided a few weeks ago to cancel the grass cutting service and do the job himself; their lawn was not so big that it warranted a fifty bucks a month outlay, and besides, it got him out of the house. Zeenah was still harboring her pre-emptive strop, convinced the call from Colton's boss was a portent of bad things to come, and she was going to lose her precious convertible. She'd barely spoken to Colton all morning, and when she did, she'd even made "pass the salt" sound like *fuck you, asshole.*

Colton pushed the lawnmower around with little enthusiasm or direction, and made random, wavy patterns in the grass. No doubt Zeenah would have something suitably snide to say about that later on, but fuck her, too. The grating, puttering noise of the lawnmower's one-and-a-half horsepower engine drowned out pretty much everything and cocooned Colton in his own little world, for which he was grateful. He figured he really ought to be worrying about what Tuesday's meeting with Mr. Christian held in store. He needed to make ready with his excuses and apologies.

But, without knowing what he was supposed to have done, how was he to know what he should be apologizing for? So, instead, Colton let his mind wander over to his dreams. Sure, Colton was smart enough to realize the world he'd created was a simple refuge he escaped to, and who could blame him really? He had a shit job—for now, anyway—a wife who clearly couldn't stand the sight of him, no friends, and a sex life in which he'd practically gone exclusive with his right hand. Textbook escapism; Colton Forshay was a walking, talking cliché.

Ah well, at least he'd have something to talk to Dr. Call-me-Zachary at his session later that afternoon. He cut the final strip of lawn and turned off the mower. He couldn't remember the last time he'd done yard work of any kind, and it felt good to have the damp feeling of an honest morning's sweat on his back. He gazed toward the house, wondering what Zeenah was up to in there. Probably drinking coffee and gossiping with her friends on the phone; she was *always* on the damned phone with her dumb friends, just what the fuck did they find to talk about?

Colton pushed the mower back into the garage and closed the door. Time for a shower, he thought, and quite possibly a small nap; cutting the grass on an empty stomach had left him a little tired.

***

The prison Colton awoke in more resembled a medieval dungeon than anything else he could bring to mind; the ones illustrated in the ancient wood-carved prints and swords-and-sorcery movies he used to love as a kid. It was built from large, gray, unevenly cut stones into which were embedded the corroded metal bars that sectioned off the cells. There was rough, prickly straw on the cold stone floor and the air was dank and stank of dampness and human sweat. Colton guessed the dungeon was most likely underground—weren't they all? And the only light was provided by a single fluorescent strip that flickered intermittently.

"You okay, Colton?" a familiar voice cut through his hazy brain. He opened his eyes and saw Eric's face smiling down at him.

"Hey," Colton said. "You're alright."

"It's gonna take more than fifty thousand volts to put this puppy down," Eric chuckled and wagged his tail.

"Good to see you, buddy." Colton scratched the special spot on his dog/son's back, the one that caused his hind leg tomake that involuntary scratching motion.

"Is that you over there, Colton?" another voice cut through the gloom. Colton sat up with a suddenness that made his head swim and his guts knot. He fought the nausea that drove the acid bile to the back of his throat and strained against the poor light to see across the hallway and into the cells opposite.

"Yeah," Colton replied.

"It's me, Cole," the voice said, and Colton's brain conjured up an image of Cole Woolston to go with the name. "Me and Honey-Lou were brought in just after you guys," Cole said, and Colton wondered if Honey-Lou Woolston was as naked and exposed as she had been at the O'Keefe's barbecue.

"Hi, Colton," Honey-Lou called out, as if on cue.

"Hey, Honey-Lou, hey Cole." Colton said, all too aware this was now sounding like the end of The Waltons.

As his eyes adjusted to the gloom, he saw movement and the dark shapes of his fellow prisoners, but was still unable to see anything solid through the dim light.

"Guess you had the dreams too?" Cole asked. "We think it was the Greens who reported us. We may have let something slip while we were snorting coke with them two nights ago."

"Those fuckers," Honey-Lou added. "And to think I let David stick that oversized cock of his up my ass." Her voice echoed a little, and Colton got that she was quite pissed at David Green. "*And* I licked Patricia's cunt out for over an hour," Honey-Lou growled. "Bitch smelled like rotten fish anyways."

Something stirred in the far corner of Colton's cell. Eric turned his head and a low growl rumbled in his throat.

"It's okay, Eric, it's only me," a scared voice offered.

"Who's me?" Eric growled as he placed himself between Colton and the unidentified person.

"Kunah, from three-o-eight," the voice said.

"Kunah Shah?" Colton enquired.

"The one and the same," Kunah ventured out from the sanctuary of the shadows, arms held out at his sides, a weak smile on his face. "How the devil are you, Colton?"

"I've been better, to be quite frank," Colton replied, the hint of a smile in his voice. "You?"

"Same, I guess," Kunah told him. "I've been in here for three weeks now, and I'm really worried about Betty."

Betty was Kunah's daughter by the Chevy Cobalt. She was a pretty young thing with loose morals; the word was she'd fuck anything with a pulse, and many things without, too.

Kunah had every right to be worried, thought Colton. Although he really couldn't bring himself to feel too much empathy for the guy; it wasn't as if they were great friends or anything. The fact was, Kunah and Colton were simply neighbors who rarely passed more than a nodded good morning on the occasion they passed on the street. Nope, they were not what Colton would call good friends.

Kunah stepped into the light, and Colton could see that he looked like Hell. His face was unshaven, and his straggly beard was matted with food and God only knew what. His clothes were grubby, sweat stained, and stank like something had died in them. Kunah held an old semen-encrusted shoe tightly in his hands—not his own footwear—which he caressed like a lover. *Such was the way of an objectophile*, Colton mused. Although he himself was hardly one to pass judgement, considering Eric.

A steel door opened somewhere in the dungeon. Its weighty, metallic *clang* reverberated around the stone walls like an exotic percussion instrument, and when it slammed shut, the finality of that sound created a feeling of deep, sickening dread amongst the five inmates.

"Oh fuck, not again," Kunah said as he shrank back into the shadows, cuddling the shoe tight to his chest. "Not again."

"What's not again?" Colton quizzed him, but Kunah remained silent.

Then, they heard the footsteps; the *clump, clump, clump* of heavy boots and an accompanying clack of what sounded very much like stiletto heels on the stone floor. A tall, flaxen-haired dominatrix strode into the stone corridor between the cells; the impossibly high heels of her black patent leather thigh-high boots beating an ominous tattoo on the chilled stones. She was blessed with a most stunning face; high cheekbones, wide, brown eyes with just a hint of an oriental slant, and fat, full lips she had accentuated with black glossy lipstick.

She wore a tight, red leather bodice that left her bountiful bosom to bounce free and display the shining gold bars pierced through her fiercely erect nipples. Her pussy was covered by a thin strap of soft black leather that snuggled deep into the groove of her vulva and left much of her outer lips exposed to show off the dark sprigs of hair that sprouted from them. Clearly, the statuesque woman was oblivious to—or immune from—the overly severe 1986 Pubic Hair Law.

The dominatrix was flanked by a burly duo of prison guards who were resplendent in their all-black uniforms and red latex face masks that obscured all but their down-turned mouths. As they marched by his cell, Colton spotted that each of the guards sported a necklace that strung down low to their hard stomachs; one was a threaded collection of dried, shrivelled penises, the other made up of what appeared to be a myriad of tiny penises but which, upon close inspection as the guards went by, were actually clitorises.

The dominatrix came to an abrupt halt at the Woolstons' cell. She waved a hand at the guard with the clitoris necklace, and he unlocked the cell with a large iron key.

"Woolston," the woman said, her voice deep and mellifluous. "Come."

"Please, no!" Cole Woolston cried out. "Not my Honey-Lou!"

"It's all okay, Cole." Honey-Lou soothed. "I promise." She stepped forward, eyes unwavering and fixed upon the dominatrix's unfettered breasts simply because they were at her eye level.

Colton peered through the gloom at Honey-Lou's brave face as she stepped forward to greet her fate with a smile. Whatever the delightful Mrs. Woolston had been doing at the time of her arrest, she had eschewed her customary nakedness in preference of a miniscule pair of gold, lame, booty shorts and a flimsy white crop top. The top revealed her toned midriff and skimmed the bottom of her tits, and the shorts clung to every line of her pussy and rode up her shapely ass to reveal almost a third of each butt cheek. Colton thought she looked heavenly.

"Take me instead!" In a fit of bravado, Cole threw himself between his wife, and the dominatrix's outstretched hand. "Please!"

Honey-Lou stepped forward again, her pretty bare feet a stark white against the dark stone of the cell floor.

The dominatrix pushed aside Honey-Lou with a large hand across the breasts. Honey-Lou flew backward and landed on her behind with a winded *oomph*.

"It's you that I have come for," the dominatrix said, her latex corset squeaking as she moved.

"Oh, shit, no!" Cole whimpered. "Please, no!" He tried to shuffle backward but had his arms grabbed by the guards.

"Bring him!" the dominatrix barked, and the guards dragged Cole from the cell.

Colton pressed his face against the bars of his cell to get a better view. Poor old Cole was fighting in vain against the strength of the two guards, his face streaming with tears. He was clad in just an off-white '*RELAX*' T-shirt, and his cock and balls swung manically as he struggled.

"Take her, not me!" Cole screamed. "She's the one having the dreams!" He wriggled again but was pulled forward by the guards, and his toes scraped raw and bloodied on the ground.

Colton saw the hurt on Honey-Lou's face; a look of betrayal yet still managing a trace of pity for her cowardly husband. At that moment, he wanted to hold her rather than fuck her.

They dragged Cole Woolston to the small, darkened antechamber at the end of the hallway. The dominatrix flicked on a switch and a single bare bulb blazed a yellow, chill light over the solid, dark wood table that dominated the room. She tore away Cole's shirt like it was made of tissue paper to render him naked and vulnerable, and he screamed hysterically.

The table was bulky and foreboding. It had wrist and ankle constraints and a pitted, blood-stained surface that told a thousand tales. Cole screamed some more when the guards hoisted him up onto the table and strapped him down. Above his head, on the damp stone wall that rose up into the seemingly endless ceiling, there was an array of vicious-looking instruments, each one crafted of rough, dark metal, and they sported razor-keen blades, cruel serrated edges or knobbly crushing surfaces. And seeing these brought forth instigated yet more hysteria from Mr. Woolston.

Colton noted with an inward shudder that many of the instruments were stained with blood. Some of it was old, dark, and flaking, some was fresher, and some had clods of rotting flesh stuck to it. And he tut-tutted under his breath; *they really ought to keep those things cleaner*, he thought; *just think of the risk of infection.* Colton also caught sight of the large circular grate—thirty inches or so in diameter—that lay the center of the room to one side of the table. The whole floor sloped slightly inward toward the drain, presumably to allow for the drainage of whatever fluids came from the table. Colton felt sick all over again.

The dominatrix dismissed the guards who clumped away back down the corridor and out of sight. She watched them go and then turned her attention to Cole.

"Please, no," he snivelled. "It was her."

"Quiet!" the dominatrix snapped. She walked around the table. Slowly, her steps deliberate, she never once took her eyes off Cole's helpless body. She flicked his flaccid penis with bony fingers adorned with long, matte black painted nails. Cole's entire body twitched, and he let out a whimper.

The dominatrix lifted her leg up onto the table, the wickedly pointed heel of her boot just a fraction of an inch from Cole's head. She lowered her crotch close to his face and pulled aside the soft leather strip that guarded her hole.

Maintaining that eye contact, she slipped two fingers inside her glistening wet pussy. Three, then four. She then folded in her thumb and her entire hand slid effortlessly into her dripping cunt. She eased her hand in and then out, in again and then out a final time with a wet slurp and a sly flick of her clit. She dropped her leg back to the floor with a loud click of heel on stone and caressed Cole's twitching dick with her slippery wet fingers.

Cole wriggled his pelvis at the woman's expert touch, and his arms and legs strained against the restraints that held him fast. He groaned from somewhere deep in his belly, and his dick began to swell as the dominatrix continued to slide her fingers along its length to coax it to full tumescence. Once this was achieved, she bent over the table and took his cock into her mouth.

Cole made a noise that sounded to Colton more like a yelp than a noise of ecstasy. He saw his neighbor's cock slide deep into the dominatrix's mouth and on down her throat to make a slight bulge in the soft skin under her angled chin. She throat fucked Cole awhile, rising and falling as his body bucked in response, and her beautiful pale cheeks indented as she sucked hard on his shaft.

Much to Cole's disappointment—Colton could see it clearly on the man's face—the dominatrix pulled her head away and continued to stroke at his cock with her hand. Cole began to pant and roll his head from side to side. His thrusting pelvic movements became more frantic and Colton figured that Cole was about to blow.

Cole grunted and thrust hard into his tormentor's hand, working hard toward his orgasm. In the blink of an eye, the dominatrix had pushed Cole's dick downward and nailed it to the wooden table by its engorged, purple head. Cole howled as his cock glans erupted in a dazzling display of pumping scarlet blood and thick white cum.

Colton staggered back from his cell bars at this, his stomach churning like a thing possessed and threatening to release his lunch. He could only presume the dominatrix had pulled the hammer and six-inch nail from the wall of tools, but he was damned if he had actually seen her do so. Eric cowered by Colton's feet, paws over his eyes, and Colton had to step over him to venture another look at Cole Woolston. He kept his hands pressed to his ears to block out the worst of Cole's agonized screams.

Blood was pouring from Cole's dick that was now very firmly pinned to the table by the thick nail. Every movement that Cole made tore at the delicate flesh and created a fresh spurt of blood, in turn causing another scream. Colton saw that the dominatrix was selecting another tool from the wall—something that looked to him like a cast-iron melon baller. Colton wanted to close his eyes but somehow his morbid fascination couldn't allow him to tear himself away.

Cole sobbed as the pain from his dick tore through his body.

"Oh, sweet Jesus, no," he cried. "I'll do anything. Please, no more."

Of course, the dominatrix ignored this meaningless plea, and taking the baller thing, she scooped out his nipples.

Cole's screams echoed throughout the prison like they were trying to beat their way through the thick walls. The tortured man's agonies were enveloping, his cries high and shrill, his pleading for mercy incomprehensible through his blubbering. And Cole's screams reached an even higher, almost inhuman pitch when the dominatrix crushed both of his balls at the same time with some kind of oversized garlic press.

Colton cringed at the sight of Cole's ruined testicles. They lay there, mashed and bloodied and dripping cloudy fluids on either side of his dick that was still pinned to the table like some exotic insect specimen. The blood and fluid that poured from Cole's balls seeped beneath his thighs and over the sides of the table where they drip-dripped in viscous threads to be swallowed up by the grate. In addition, Cole's chest was a bright red mess of blood that welled up fresh and slick from the carved semi circles where his nipples had once sat; that, too, made its way to the grate.

The dominatrix reached up high above her head and pulled from the wall a blood-stained pair of tongs that boasted a particularly unpleasant looking set of ragged metal teeth. She plunged the tongs into Cole's screaming mouth, gripped his tongue and pulled. Cole's head jerked upward as far as it would go given the straps that held his wrists. Cole strained to move upward with the tongs until the muscles and tendons in his neck stood taut, but he could go no further. The dominatrix smiled into Cole's terror-widened eyes as she stretched his tongue fully out of his mouth until the flesh that held it in his mouth began to rip with an audible tearing sound not unlike that of expensive silk. Blood spurted from Cole's mouth and sprayed the dominatrix's swollen breasts with such volume that it dripped back onto him from her pointed nipples.

Another swift motion—she was good at those—and the dominatrix removed Cole's tongue at the root with a paring knife. She held the tongue aloft for him to see, and Cole screamed as best he could with no tongue and a mouth filled with blood. He struggled and bucked on the table and coughed and spluttered thick gobs of blood over his ruined body, his cries wet and gurgling. The dominatrix, in what appeared to be an uncharacteristically tender gesture, twisted Cole's head to one side to allow the blood from his mouth to pour out, presumably to prevent him drowning in the stuff.

The dominatrix ran the paring knife along the center of Cole's chest from throat to belly. The keen knife blade left a fresh trail of red through which the white bone of its victim's sternum glinted. The dominatrix continued on with the knife, downward to where, with a deft flick of the wrist, she severed Cole's penis at its base. The severed dick flopped to the table with a wet *plop,* and thick blood seeped out from the neatly sliced end; although it was liberated from Cole's body, the deflating dick remained nailed firmly to the table.

Cole's agonized protests were rapidly diminishing. The loss of such a volume blood and the assault in his senses of such intense pain were draining him both physically and mentally. He groaned and pulled at the wrist and ankle restraints with less vigor as his body began to close down and give up the will to live.

"Mrs. Woolston?" the dominatrix's voice rose above her victim's gurgles. "Come."

Colton glanced across at the cell opposite; he'd forgotten that poor Honey-Lou was in there, hearing everything he was hearing, seeing everything he could see. He saw that she was sitting on the stone floor of her cell as she watched the spectacle of her husband's torture. Her legs were spread akimbo, tight shorts pulled to one side and she was masturbating. He watched, mesmerized as Honey-Lou's fingers rubbed furiously away at her clitoris, only breaking rhythm to slide knuckle-deep into the pink swollen folds of her cunt.

Honey-Lou came with an ear-splitting squeal, her orgasm so intense it made her body judder. From his vantage point, Colton could see her feet twitch and dance and her breasts quiver, and it made him hard.

"Now," the dominatrix demanded.

Honey-Lou replaced the gusset of her slinky shorts over her swollen sex and struggled to her feet, her wobbly legs threatening mutiny as she did so. She made her way past Colton's cell without so much as a glance at its occupants, her entire attention focused on the writhing wreck that was her husband.

"It is time to say goodbye," the Dominatrix said as she held the paring knife out for Honey-Lou to take.

"No." Honey-Lou shook her head. Her face was still sweaty and flushed pink from her orgasm, her voice croaky and raw.

"It's your choice, Honey-Lou," the dominatrix purred. "Either you deliver the *coup de grace* now, or I keep him alive and in unspeakable agony for days, perhaps even weeks."

She drew the knife along Cole's right thigh. The skin parted, and the knife slid deep into the meat of his quad muscle. Blood began to pour from the wound, and Cole writhed in pain.

"Please, stop it," Honey-Lou sobbed.

"This man tried to give you up to save himself," the dominatrix spat. "What kind of a husband does that?" She traced a line on Cole's chest, just below the blood-clotted hole where his left nipple used to be, and then crossed through it with another. Blood flowed free and bright from the cross shape she'd drawn on Cole's chest, and he screamed the best he could with no tongue. Cole rocked his head from side to side, and his eyes implored his wife to bring him escape from the torment.

"Come along now," the dominatrix coaxed with a wicked sparkle in her eye and a faint smile on her night-black lips. "X marks the spot." She held the knife out across the table, across Cole Woolston.

And Honey-Lou took hold of it.

Honey-Lou stared the dominatrix hard in the eyes, her hatred clear and focused. She saw the woman had a second knife; an unpleasant looking thing with a long, serrated blade that curved upward.

"If you are thinking of doing something heroic, I'd suggest you think again, Honey-Lou," the dominatrix growled. "I could have a lot of fun with you on this table. Give you two, three weeks in my expert hands, and you'd be begging me to finish you." A smile. "If you are a good girl, however, and do what really needs to be done here, then I will make your demise quick and painless." A light laugh. "Relatively speaking, of course."

Cole did his best to shout "*no*" at his wife but succeeded only in coughing thick clots of dark blood over himself, and his face became a bloodied mask.

"Look at him, Honey-Lou," the dominatrix urged. "No tongue, no dick. What use is he to you now? What use is he to anyone? He'd just be a burden, unable to satisfy his woman or pay his way." Her voice purred with a sensual lilt that made Honey-Lou wet in spite of herself; she could feel her warm juice soaking through her shorts. "And who would want to live like that?"

Honey-Lou plunged the knife into her husband's chest, a precise hit in the centre of the bloodied X that the dominatrix had drawn there. Cole let out a gargled shriek of surprise and went into a wild spasm as the keen metal blade sliced into his heart. Bright blood bubbled out around the knife's hilt, soaking Honey-Lou's hand and pooling in Cole's navel.

"I am so sorry, my lover," Honey-Lou wept.

Cole Woolston died with his eyes wide with an accusing stare, his mouth agape and filled with clotting blood. For Honey-Lou, it was a relief when her husband finally quit wriggling around on the table, and she could pull out the knife. It slipped out of Cole with a faint sucking sound, and she could feel it snag on his ribs as she pulled.

"And now it's your turn." The dominatrix sidled up to Honey-Lou and took the knife from her hand with no resistance. "I promised I would make it quick, and I always keep my promises." She stroked Honey-Lou's smooth head with a fond smile and slipped her hand downward to caress her exposed lower back as she lifted the curved knife to Honey-Lou's throat.

Honey-Lou closed her eyes, anticipating the cool blade of the dominatrix's knife, desperate to shut out the sight of her husband's ruined corpse and the reality of her own impending death.

The sting of the knife blade never came.

Honey-Lou felt the dominatrix's hand fall away from her back, heard a sighed '*oh*' and the woman's warm breath on her face. And when she heard the raw, grating sound of metal on stone, Honey-Lou Woolston opened her eyes.

The grate in the center of the room was being pushed aside but all Honey-Lou could see was a large pair of hands maneuvering the metal cover, and another hand holding what appeared to be a long, silver sword. Her eye followed the glinting blade upward from its ornate hilt and saw that sword had been thrust up into the dominatrix. It had entered her body between vagina and anus, and exited through her left breast, one would presume, via her heart. The dominatrix stood, frozen, as if refusing to believe she was dying. Her mouth opened and closed as if she were trying to say something as a thin trickle of blood snaked down from the exit wound on her tit.

Three men clambered out from the inky darkness. They were dressed head-to-foot in black overalls, their faces smeared with black paint and with them came the stench of the sewers. The dominatrix turned her head to face her killer, that incredulous look still in her eyes, and she attempted to scream. The noise that came from her throat reminded Honey-Lou of Cole's final gargling grunts; an odd, liquid gurgle.

The guy holding the sword pulled it out of the dominatrix, and she slumped to the floor with blood pouring from the wide but neat slice in her perineum to pool around her body.

"Looks like we were just in time," Sword Guy said as he placed a comforting arm around Honey-Lou's shoulders. "I am so sorry about your husband." He glanced at Cole's body, gave it a resigned look and patted Honey-Lou on the butt. "If there was anything we could do, we would, but …" he paused, and his face said it all. "We have to get out of here." He nodded to one of his men to escort the distraught Honey-Lou to the ladder that now protruded from the hole in the floor, and he strode with purpose toward Colton's cell.

Colton and Eric were skulking in the protection of the shadows that enveloped the rear of the cell, along with Kunah and his shoe. They had retreated there once things started getting really nasty with the dominatrix, keen to shut out the sights and sounds of what they assumed would be their fate once the sadistic woman had had her fun with Cole Woolston and his poor wife.

So, the sound of a key in the cell door lock sent chills along Colton's spine, and he murmured a prayer to a God that he only half believed in.

"Come with me," a voice in the gloom said as the cell door swung open. "Quickly."

"Don't do it, Colton," Eric urged. "You saw what happened to Cole." He placed a paw on Colton's leg.

"This is a rescue attempt, asshole," the voice said. "There'll be time for explanations later, but we're leaving now, with or without you." And he stepped to where Colton could see his face.

"Zachary?" Colton sputtered.

"Please, call me Zack." The familiar face said with a puzzled smile.

***

Colton's eyes snapped open to find he was in the all-too-familiar shrink's office.

"Zack?" Colton said as his eyes focused on Dr. Stackhouse.

"Zachary, please," Stackhouse was insistent. He leaned forward in his overstuffed chair, fingers entwined in the way primary school kids play *steeple*. "Well, Colton," he said. "It is becoming quite clear to me your dreams are an obvious compensation for what you see as lacking in your physical relationship with your wife." He leaned back again, and Colton thought he looked smug.

No fucking shit, Sherlock. Colton's mind ranted. *Like I needed to pay a hundred fifty bucks an hour to hear that.*

"Given the overtly sexual nature of your dreams, I'd say that you were creating this nameless dream world of yours to fulfill your fantasies that Zeenah can—or will—not." Again, that half-smile that could easily be self-satisfaction. "Although, it is worrisome that you appear to be functioning whilst in a dream state."

He was right about that one, although worrisome wasn't the word Colton would have applied there. Downright shit scary was how he saw it; as a prime example, he had no recollection of getting to the shrink's office or anything that may have transpired upon arrival.

"How much have I told you?" Colton asked.

"Most of it, I think," Stackhouse replied. "But one question; who is Eric?"

Colton stared openmouthed at the shrink. No idea where to begin on that one. Regaling the man with tales of sexual debauchery was one thing but explaining how he'd made offspring with his pet dog—albeit in a dream—was another.

"Perhaps that's one for our next session," Stackhouse glanced at his watch.

"Perhaps," Colton replied. He was still somewhat nonplussed at having Stackhouse pop up in his dreams as some kind of action-hero person—was there no getting away from this guy? Colton stood up from the couch, made ready to leave.

"Your wife called, Colton," the shrink told him. "I didn't want to say anything before our session, didn't want you preoccupied."

"Zeenah called?"

"Yes, she called me because she is concerned about what you did before you left the house to come here." Stackhouse adopted his worried face. "And, quite frankly, I can understand how she feels."

"What did I do?" Colton experienced a weird tingle in his lower guts that felt like his balls were trying to crawl back up in there.

"I think you should go home and discuss that with your wife, Colton," Stackhouse told him.

Was that a look of judgement or disgust on the shrink's face? Colton couldn't be sure, so he said nothing further and he left.

CHAPTER SIX

"So, you see, Colton." Mr. Christian said. The old man peered down his spectacles at Colton as if he were some mildly interesting insect. "This is a very serious situation."

"I understand, Mr. Christian." Colton remained passive, not sure what the reply should be. He stared across the round table at his boss, then across to Stacey Williamson: Barnett, Schuster, and Wolfe's stalwart of the Human Resource department. A blanched-face, rotund woman of indeterminate but advanced years, Stacey had been with the company since its inception back in the darkest mists of time.

Brought out the big guns eh, Christian? There must be some really serious shit going down.

Colton fought to maintain his composure, even though his heart was pounding hard and fast in his chest, his mouth was as dry as a lizard's ass, and his head was racing. Obviously, he'd done something pretty dire last Friday afternoon. Something that warranted his first trip to HR since he'd started at the company five years ago—but what? Colton cleared his throat, although he had nothing to say, other than this was the last fucking thing he needed in his life right now, and could they please cut to the chase as the suspense was killing him?

He was still reeling somewhat from the verbal assault that awaited him upon return from his appointment with Stackhouse. Zeenah had been sitting on the couch in *that* silence, lips pursed, arms folded across her chest, and a steely look in her eye. He'd barely gotten across the threshold before she'd launched her attack, screaming at him in that frenetic pitch that always made his ears hurt, and she'd called him every bad name she could think of.

"Asshole! Pervert! Fucking deviant! Sick Bastard! Cunt!"

And all Colton had been able to do was stand there and take it like some shell-shocked mute and wait 'till she'd calmed down enough to explain the crimes that warranted such venomous verbal abuse.

It transpired that, prior to his trip out to see Dr. Stackhouse, and following his post lawn-cutting shower, Colton had seen fit to put on Zeenah's most expensive pair of lace panties and sneak up behind her whilst she was talking to yet another of her friends on the phone. He'd tapped her on the shoulder, and when she turned around to see what it was he wanted, Colton had stuck his erect penis into her mouth.

Penis. She'd actually called it that to his face. Zeenah never said the p-word, hated it in fact. Throughout their marriage, it had always been *thing, thingy, whatnot, manhood,* and on occasion, in the throes of drunken passion, *dick.* According to his wife's version of events—and that was all Colton had to go on as he had absolutely no recollection of anything that afternoon—he had ejaculated almost instantaneously into her mouth and then turned and simply walked away. He'd left her there with it dribbling from the corner of her dumbfounded mouth with her friend's distant, metallic voice shouting concerned hellos from the receiver. Colton had been out of the house before Zeenah had regained her composure enough to react, hence the phone call to the shrink.

After the verbal kicking, Zeenah had subjected him to the silent treatment; that eerie nothingness in which neither party knows what not to say. In some ways, this was far worse than the verbal abuse; at least then they were communicating. Whilst he had not been relegated to the couch, Colton had been forced to endure the further torment of the gaping, cold chasm between he and his wife in bed, which actually made the couch seem preferable.

"We have had several complaints, plus we have the footage from the security camera." Stacey Williamson cut across Colton's thoughts. She spun her laptop around and hit the return key.

Colton squinted at the grainy black and white footage; saw himself making a phone call. The footage—obviously edited to cut out the more boring parts—jumped forward in time a half hour or so to show Colton welcoming a statuesque black lady with long, shiny black hair into his cubicle.

Colton held his head in his hands as the drama unfolded on the screen. He watched as the black lady undressed, first herself, and then Colton; he saw three of his colleagues from the accounts floor walk by and peer into his cubicle. And as he watched, the black lady turned around and—

"It would appear you invited a transsexual prostitute into our offices, Mr. Forshay," Christian said.

And indeed, he had.

The hooker wielded a cock of the most formidable proportions. It sprang out of his tight underpants with all the eagerness of a puppy ready to play. The hooker then produced an impressive amount of cocaine from his sequinned purse, which both he and Colton snorted from Colton's workstation.

"I think you can see just how serious this transgression is, Colton," Stacey added. "You are lucky we haven't called in the police."

"I appreciate that, Mrs. Williams. Thank you," Colton said as he watched his monochrome self bend over his desk to take the full length of the hooker's impressive dick up his ass.

"There are so many violations of company code here, Colton," Christian informed him. "We really don't know where to start."

On the laptop screen, Colton saw a third figure appear and recognised her as Gabrielle Lacour, the shy, frumpy woman from bookkeeping. She slipped into the cubicle and without further ado, began to undress. Once down to her smalls, she sprinkled cocaine onto the hooker's muscular butt cheeks, rolled up a hundred and snorted it from the guy's sweating skin as he fucked Colton.

"Gabrielle?" Colton muttered.

"Rest assured, we will be taking the appropriate disciplinary action with Miss Lacour later on today," Stacey said with a snide tone to her voice that Colton didn't much care for. Was the snooty bitch judging him here? Was she enjoying watching the porn show he'd put on whilst his mind had been elsewhere? Was she getting all wet and unnecessary in her ancient vag' right now, desperate to nip off to the unisex restrooms to flick a finger or two over the old dusty peanut?

"This really is no laughing matter, Colton," Christian picked up on Colton's wry smile. "There really is only one course of action available to us, I'm afraid."

And here it came, *The Inevitable*. So why spend all this time watching the Colton Forshay, Bisexual, Drug-Fuelled

Fuckshow when they were just going to fire his pervert ass anyway? Christian—sorry, *Mr. Christian*—could have just as simply done that over the phone on Friday night.

Colton stood up.

"You know what?" he said. "Fuck you, the both of you." He smiled. "Yeah, fuck both of you."

And with that, Colton strode from the office.

***

There really was no point in him going home to Zeenah. Although Colton knew he was just delaying the inevitable, he simply couldn't face his wife and her harpy voice right now. He had no intention of telling her the why, but he was resigned to the fact he would have to give her the news of his sacking from Barnett, Schuster, and Wolfe, which would no doubt lead to yet more shouting and accusations. She'd find out sooner or later the *why*, but Colton decided to leave that big reveal to the office grapevine. Zeenah was friends with a few of the girls in customer relations, and his actions last Friday were the stuff office legends were made of. It was bound to get out to Zeenah before long; gossip that juicy simply *couldn't* stay buried.

It was still early, the bars would not be open for another hour, and his favorite brothel was closed on Tuesdays, so Colton decided to head to the park. At least there, he could take some time out to himself to sit in the sunshine and think things through

Colton found a bench not spotted with pigeon crap and sat himself down. The morning sun was pleasantly warm on his face, and the gentle breeze not too cooling to prevent him from removing his jacket. The park was almost empty as regular (employed) folk were at work this time of the day. The only souls Colton saw were a homeless woman sleeping off her night's excesses and an elderly man walking an equally elderly dog. Watching the dog as it waddled along in that ungainly side-to-side of old, overweight canines, Colton's mind turned to Eric.

Who is Eric?

Colton found it remarkable that, despite having related just about every detail about his dreams—ironically, whilst in a dream state—to Dr. Stackhouse, Colton had omitted an explanation of Eric. And somehow, this made Colton feel like he'd betrayed his own flesh and blood. Like he'd denied Eric as the disciples had denied their Christ. This, he found, was more disturbing to him than Stackhouse's intrusion in his dreams, although Colton knew he only had his own imagination to blame for putting the man there in the first place.

Memories of his dreams stayed fresh and vivid in Colton's mind. He could picture faces, hear voices, smell the alien scents as if they had been real and right in front of him. And, most disturbing of all for Colton, he was beginning to find himself retreating into the dream world whenever things got tough here in the real world. And even he knew just how unhealthy that was for a grown man, especially now he'd just got his pink slip.

Colton mused on how he would nowadays catch himself thinking about the dream conversations he'd had, imagining new ones, even missing the weird and wonderful people who populated his dream world. And most of all, how he missed all the bizarre and exciting sex those people symbolized. Colton reckoned he ought to really be more concerned about the fact his dreams were slowly, but surely, creeping in on his everyday life, but that didn't seem to bother him so much. Although, that was not to say he had full licence to lay the blame for his recent behavior that had pissed off his wife and cost him his job squarely at the feet of his dreams. Stackhouse had hit a nail on the head with that one, given the overtly sexual nature of his dreams and his subsequent actions. What really was of concern here, Colton reminded himself, was that he was having the dreams *and* living his life, at the same time.

Now, that wasn't normal.

It certainly gave food for thought and was most likely, Colton thought, *to be the subject of Dr. Zachary Stackhouse's next published paper in the Psychiatric Review or whatever shrink's periodical he subscribed to.*

Nail on the head.

Now, that phrase had set off a chain reaction in Colton's mind, which began with poor old Cole Woolston with the six inches of ironmongery hammered through his mangled meatus and ending with his own descent on the rickety ladder into those dark, stinking sewers beneath the prison.

Colton then began to wonder if it was possible to rejoin his dream world at will, something he had yet to try—there'd been no reason to thus far. To be truthful, he had found himself missing his dream world since his last sojourn, and in light of today's bombshell, the thought of a little escapism would be most welcome. Colton closed his eyes, enjoyed the warmth of the sun's rays on his eyelids, and willed himself to doze as he wondered where he'd pick up.

***

"Do I know you?" Zack asked Colton, a direct question that would solicit a far from direct reply.

"Err, no. I don't think so," Colton stammered as he struggled for the right words.

Zack was driving a black SUV, his hands gripping the steering wheel with such ferocity his knuckles had turned white. He steered the SUV off the deserted main road they were on—it looked to Colton that the prison had been in the middle of nowhere—and onto a narrow side road toward the gas station he somehow knew was a couple of miles along.

In the eight-seater with Zack rode Colton, Eric, a traumatised Honey-Lou Woolston, Kunah (plus shoe), and the two black-clad guys who had helped him bust the motley selection of individuals from the prison. Zack had wasted little time in introducing himself as leader of the Resistance; the courageous body of men and women who fought tirelessly against the government's persecution of those who had *the dream*—his words, not Colton's. As it transpired, Colton was far from unique in his dreams of the Other Place, which he thought amusing, given the circumstances.

The Resistance lay blame for the violent repression of the people they had given the uninspired epithet *The Dreamers* at the president's door; there was clearly something in those dreams, so the thinking went, that so terrified President Ocelot, that he was forced to torture and kill anyone who confessed to having them. Although, no one had yet figured out exactly what that something could be.

"Which is why we have been planning our next move," Zack hinted. "And why we need good people—*Dreamers*—like you guys."

"Next move?" Eric asked. "What's that?"

"Can't say just now, there are ears everywhere." Zack pointed through the sunroof, at the sky. "There are satellites up there that can hear an ant fart."

"Ants fart?" Honey-Lou said. This was the first thing she'd uttered since their rescue, and everyone just looked at her and smiled. She looked so small and fragile, yet still damned sexy.

"Just a turn of phrase, Ma'am," Zack explained. "You sure we've never met?" He turned his attention back to Colton.

Colton smiled and assured him that no, they had never met, and marvelled to himself at just how accurately his dream had recreated his psychiatrist as a hero of the piece.

"I do know you in my—my *other place*," Colton ventured.

"You mean, in your dream place?" Zack corrected him.

"No, err, yeah, I guess so. Only, there, this is the dream place," Colton told him. "And there, you're my shrink."

"Me!? A shrink!" Zack laughed. "And here's me thinking it was all white picket fences, football tailgating, and Mom's apple pie." He laughed a hearty laugh and his two sidekicks laughed along.

"You mean you don't dream the dreams?" Honey-Lou said.

"Hell no!" Zack guffawed. "I'm just the guy who helps you guys that do!" He cackled to himself for a mile or so and then fell once more into silence.

Colton went back to staring out the window, and Zack pulled the vehicle into the service station forecourt and eased the SUV to a halt.

The elderly pump attendant shuffled out from the ramshackle trailer office that doubled as a small store. "Howdy," he greeted and doffed his tattered Red Sox cap. Colton, Zack, and Eric got out of the SUV, keen to stretch their aching legs.

"Fill her up," Zack instructed and made his way to the port-a-potty restroom at the side of the trailer. The attendant nodded and unzipped his oil-stained pants.

"Shandene!" the old man called out with a phlegm-clogged voice. "We got customers!" He pulled out his penis, opened the gas flap and began to pee into the gas tank with a strong, steady stream. "If ya'd like to get one of your friends ta' pop the hood?" he asked Colton and pointed at Zack's associates who sat inside staring out at him.

Colton mouthed *hood,* and one of the guys leaned over the driver's seat and pulled the lever.

A pretty young girl, whom Colton assumed to be Shandene, appeared. Colton stared at her, slack-jawed, as she sashayed toward the SUV and felt his dick swell to uncomfortable proportions in his pants. Shandene was wearing only a pair of grubby sneakers and the most miniscule bikini Colton had ever set his eyes upon. The bikini was constructed of little more than metallic blue string; it sure as hell looked as if whoever had made it had forgotten to add the material. The string gave the resemblance of the outline of the iconic swimsuit, but left her small, pert breasts bare and served only as an outline to the thin slit of her pussy.

Shandene smiled at Colton.

"Howdy," she said, her voice smooth, seductive.

"Hi," was all Colton could manage to utter. Most of his attention was split equally between the girl's beautifully displayed body and the ache in his dick. He looked down at Eric and saw that he too, was transfixed by the girl and was getting more than a little aroused himself.

As they watched, Shandene lifted the SUV's hood, climbed up onto the front of the car and positioned herself over the hot engine block. Colton noted that, from the back, the girl looked completely naked—the rear straps of the bikini were even thinner than those at the front and were made of a clear, plastic material.

Before Colton knew what was happening, he found himself watching the girl in the bikini made entirely from strings fingering her pussy at an alarming speed over the engine block. Clear, viscous strings of her vaginal secretions poured from her body and roped down to sizzle on the hot engine.

"I really didn't need the oil change," Zack said as he emerged from the restroom, totally unphased by the girl.

"That's okay," the old man told him. "Oil's on the house." He stood back from the car, closed the gas flap with one hand and tucked his wrinkled cock back into his pants with the other.

Shandene finished up her own job in hand and flicked the last viscous threads of her juices onto the engine with a flourish before she climbed back down and closed the hood.

"That'll be one ass-fucking, please," the attendant said. He unbuckled his belt and his pants fell to his ankles. He pulled down his faded boxer shorts and dropped to all fours, his withered old rump offered high in the air.

"Would you mind getting this, Colton, buddy," Zack slapped Colton on the shoulder. "I would, but I had to bribe a guard or two at the prison, and you know how it is."

Colton sighed. Yes, he did know how it is, and had he been required to pay the delicious Shandene for services rendered, there'd be no problem. But now, staring down at the liver-spotted, wrinkled old butthole of the attendant, he found his ardor somewhat diminished.

"It's okay," Eric stepped forward, his face smiling up at Colton. "I got this." And with that, he mounted the attendant. Eric's bulbous dog-dick stuck out and proud, an angry, shiny red that contrasted splendidly against both his brindle coat and the old man's pasty backside.

Colton couldn't bring himself to watch Eric's cock slithering in and out of the old man's saggy ass, and since Shandene had taken that magnificent body of hers back into the trailer, Colton decided to get back into the vehicle. They all waited patiently for Eric to finish up paying the attendant, which he did so with a joyful howl. He padded back to the SUV and climbed in. Zack gunned the engine and pulled away from the gas station.

"Thank you," Colton said.

"My absolute pleasure." Eric replied. "And his." He nodded toward the attendant who stood waving them goodbye with his pants down, shrivelled dick in hand, and a thick dribble of Eric's semen running down the inside of his thigh.

The remainder of the trip was uneventful as it seemed everyone in the SUV preferred to retreat back into their own thoughts, none more so than Colton. Somewhere between the gas station and the Resistance headquarters—it was difficult to tell as the highway was just one long straight road of featureless monotony—Honey-Lou cuddled up to Colton, nestled her petite body into his. Colton draped his arm around her and enjoyed the warmth of her body next to his.

****

Zack got them all to their destination around sundown. The clouds hung heavy in the dusk sky, stained salmon pink by the slowly sinking sun, and the cicadas buzzed shrill and loud in the trees that overhung the driveway he turned the SUV on to. Relieved to be free of the confines of the SUV, Zack's passengers climbed out and stretched their stiffened limbs, groaning at the effort. Colton stared up at the imposing gray, stone-built building that stretched before him, batted away a fat bodied mosquito that buzzed around his face.

The Resistance HQ had been originally built as out of town offices for a reclusive software company that had gone bust a month or two before the building could be completed. That was when the ass end fell out of the dotcom market. The Resistance had taken it over a couple of years ago and had finished off the building work and then furbished the office block to suit their own needs. It now resembled a cross between a modern office block and an eighteenth-century English manor house, which Colton considered to be a particularly unholy mix.

Unsightly as it was, the building more than suited the requirements of the Resistance both in respect of its impressive size and its location in the middle of a five-thousand-acre ranch in the middle of nowhere. It was perfect for the gathering of individuals wanted by the government and known criminals who wanted to strategize their nefarious plans in secret.

A valet appeared as if from nowhere and whisked the SUV and Zack's henchmen away to the vast underground parking garage, leaving the five remaining passengers to make their way toward the imposing entryway.

"This place is awesome," Honey-Lou gasped as they entered the vestibule, straining her neck up to gawk at the high vaulted ceiling.

"Wow," Kunah joined in, his eye settling on an ornate vase that stood at almost a man's height in the corner. He dropped his shoe and shuffled over to the vase, and he began to lick it.

"Welcome to the Pleasuredome, people," Zack announced with pride.

Colton followed Zack, Eric padding by his side with his nails click-clacking on the marble floor. Honey-Lou held tight onto Colton's hand; so hard, in fact, Colton could feel his phalanges grind against one another.

As they walked along a hallway that appeared to go on forever and deep into the heart of the building, Zack explained to Colton and the others that the Resistance building was an eclectic mix of living quarters, conference rooms, and play areas. Everything was powered by an impressive bank of generators in the basement, and the building was completely self sufficient in water as it had an endless supply from an artesian well somewhere beneath the expansive grounds.

"We are big enough to be able to offer a secure refuge for the persecuted," Zack added. "As well as living quarters for the soldiers of the Resistance."

"Play areas?" Eric enquired. "You said there were play areas."

"Yes, I did, buddy," Zack smiled. "All work and no play and all of that." He rubbed the fur on Eric's back the wrong way, and Eric wagged his tail.

They finally reached the end of the hallway, for which Colton was grateful because his legs had started to ache, and he really needed to pee (should have gone at the gas station, but didn't want to miss Shandene and her delightful cunt). Zack paused at an impressive pair of solid oak doors ornately carved with delightful woodland scenes complete with deer, squirrels, the wildest of wild boars, and naked, heavy-breasted wood nymphs.

"There's a full briefing for the Big Plan at eleven-hundred hours in conference room four," he said. "You will all need to be there. You will be allocated sleeping quarters very shortly." He pulled open the heavy doors with a grunt. "In the meantime, enjoy."

The doors swung open to reveal the cavernous room beyond. The room was filled with naked people and illuminated with low light like some vast, sensual boudoir. The walls were adorned with striking diaphanous silks and erotic portraiture that depicted every sexual act one could possibly think of, and some besides. Colton breathed deep to take in the sensuous smells of exotic perfumes and intense sex and rejoiced at the sweet sounds of orgasmic ecstasy of the innumerable people in the throes of pleasure.

"Sweet mother of God," Colton mumbled as his senses were caressed by the utopia before him.

And before he knew what was happening, Honey-Lou was pulling him by the hand into the room with the broadest, hungriest of smiles on her elfin face.

CHAPTER SEVEN

Somehow, somewhere between the doorway and twenty feet or so into the expansive room, Honey-Lou Woolston had gotten naked. To Colton's surprise, she'd managed to shed her clothes whilst he had been marvelling at the playroom; probably not a difficult task considering just how mesmerized Colton was by the sights, sounds, and smells of the room, and also the minimalism of Honey-Lou's outfit. Resplendent and confident in her bareness, she pulled on Colton's arm to lead him into the bosom of the fantastical place that brimmed with sexual desires.

There were oversized beds everywhere one looked. Each one was dressed with crisp white sheets and upon most there were naked, writhing bodies in any and every conceivable combination. On one, a solitary lady lay spread-eagled and surrounded by at least twenty young men. The eager men stroked and caressed her body as she squirmed with pleasure. One of the men slid his penis into her vagina, another one into her ass, and she cried out in pained ecstasy as the two fucked her to orgasm with their balls slapping together. The other participants rubbed and ground their stiff dicks over every inch of her body, in her face, and in her long, blonde hair. She spied Colton and smiled at him, held out a hand for him to join in with her fantasy, but Honey-Lou pulled him away.

"I'll bet the good stuff is over here," she giggled. She led Colton swiftly past the woman on the bed, and she delighted in fondling the firm asses of several of the young men as she went by.

At the end of the playroom were a series of doors. They were smaller than the main doors into the room, but solid oak and impressive, nonetheless. As people made their way in and out of the doors, Colton caught tantalizing glimpses of the erotic pleasures that dwelled within, and he had an idea that Honey-Lou might just be right.

Colton allowed Honey-Lou to lead him on, happy to go with her flow as she seemed to have a nose for the more superlative sexual activities. They skirted by a bed that swarmed with copulating couples; their limbs were tangled and entwined, uncountable fingers probing, tongues exploring, and he inhaled deeply to enjoy the musky scents of sex that wafted from the melee. Honey-Lou squeezed herself and Colton between yet another two beds, one of which housed two blonde girls who appeared to be conjoined twins. Colton paused to stare, and they smiled at him. He could see that they were joined at their four-breasted chest and that they shared three arms, the middle one of which reached out to Colton in invitation. The twins twisted their heads to face one another and kissed hard and deep, their wrestling tongues invaded each other's mouth. Their busy hands grasped at the breasts they shared, kneading at the soft, liquid flesh and tweaking roughly at the jutting, aroused nipples that sprouted from them. The girls' middle arm snaked downward along their smooth torso and sank its stubby fingers into one of the pussies and then switched to the other and then back again, becoming wetter with each dalliance.

Eric appeared as if from nowhere and jumped up onto the bed, his dick erect and free of its sheath. The girls giggled and pulled him to their bosom with fingers that dug into the thick fur of his back.

"I'll be right here if you need me," Eric smiled at Colton. "You kids go have yourselves some fun."

Honey-Lou pulled Colton away from the delightfully sensual twins and into one of the side rooms. Left to his own devices, Colton would have been quite content to have made his own entertainment in the main room, but the sight of Honey-Lou's trim, tanned body, pert, pierced tits, delicious pussy lips and those eyes that twinkled with deviant promise had made him putty in her hands. Right now, he knew he would have followed the girl to hell and back.

The room they found themselves in was bare and a stark contrast to the plush decor on the other side of its thick, wooden door. The walls were bare plaster, the floor rough concrete, and the room was lit by a pair of fluorescent strip lights that hummed overhead. In the dead center of the room was a large wooden chair that was streaked with blood—old and new—and was bolted to the floor. Standing around the chair were three people; a large, muscular guy with tribal tattoos adorning his arms and thick thighs, a thick-set, middle aged woman with pendulous, National Geographic tits, and a stunning redheaded girl with red rose tattoos that covered the entire left side of her curvaceous body from her calves to her neck. All three were naked, of course, and were paying great attention to the occupant of the chair. As the trio turned to greet Colton and Honey-Lou, they parted, and Colton recognized the guy in the chair.

"David Green?" Colton exclaimed.

David looked at Colton with sad, pained eyes, unable to return Colton's greeting because the naked people had sewn his lips together. Colton could see that someone had carved *SNITCH* into his chest and blood dripped from each letter like it was a 1980's horror movie font.

"He's the one who had us arrested?" Honey-Lou let go of Colton's hand and circled the chair.

"You and many others," Muscular guy said. "And now he's finding out what happens to informers." He turned to fully face Colton, his semi-erect penis so magnificently long and thick that Colton almost gasped.

"I think he's ready," the redhead announced. She stepped back to admire her handiwork and Colton noticed that each of the hand-sized blooms inked on the girl's flank was made up of plump labia.

Redhead produced a razor blade from somewhere about her person and made great theatre of unwrapping it from its paper packet in front of David Green's terrified eyes. She then used the blade to flay David Green's entire front from the dip at the bottom of his throat to his navel. All the while, David struggled against the restraints and screamed the best he could against the thick cotton that held his lips tightly shut. Within minutes, David's skin was gone, and raw, seeping flesh had taken its place; blood dribbled down into his lap and pooled around his penis, which was, in spite of itself, fully erect.

The flabby middle-aged woman tickled the head of David's dick, made it twitch to attention. David moaned, almost beyond pain now.

"Bring her in," she raised her voice.

Colton looked around as the door opened once more and a couple made their way in, carrying between them a tightly bound and gagged figure. The couple were clad in red leather outfits, he in chaps and a vest, she in a tight leotard with an open crotch. Between them, they carried Patricia

Green who had been bound in traditional Japanese rope bondage style with rough hemp rope that had chafed her skin into seeping open sores. As they carried Patricia towards her husband, her eyes locked with Colton's. Unable to so much as wriggle, she tried to scream against the ball gag that filled her mouth but achieved nothing more discernible than a muffled *hmmmmmm hmmmpf mmmm*. Colton shook his head; it was sad to see Patricia like this, and he remembered fondly the last time he'd seen her; resplendent in latex and rubbing herself to a screaming orgasm on Elizabeth Venegas's blubbery leg.

The leather-clad couple knelt Patricia at her husband's feet, and she stared up at his skinned body with tearful eyes as if feeling his pain along with her own.

Redhead maneuvered herself behind Patricia, her hand clutching the razor blade that she'd used to strip David of his skin. She wiped the silver blade clean on her thigh, which left a thin smear of David's blood on her alabaster skin.

Middle-aged woman grabbed hold of David's dick and smiled as it twitched with involuntary pleasure. Honey-Lou clung to Colton, her body pressed tight to his side. Colton could feel her fidgeting, and he knew that she was grinding her thighs together. He looked down at her and caught the sweet scent of her arousal sweat and moist sex.

The redhead girl drew the razor across Patricia's throat, and it opened up with a fountain of blood that gushed onto David's crotch. Colton cringed at this sudden show of brutality, sickened that he could see Patricia's feet twitching as if she were trying to run away.

David screamed his muffled scream and thick snot bubbled from his nose. He rolled his head and closed his eyes against the horrors happening to him as Redhead pushed Patricia forward, and the middle-aged woman forced his dick into the gash in Patricia's throat.

"Now fuck her," Muscle man growled into David's ear. David shook his head *no* so Muscleman slapped his victim's raw chest hard, and David squealed behind his sealed lips.

"I said, fuck her. Before she's too damned dead to enjoy it."

And David Green began to thrust his cock in and out of his wife's gurgling trachea, each thrust tipping her head backwards and forcing more blood to bubble out.

Colton had seen enough and left the room, pulling with him a reluctant Honey-Lou. Unlike his companion who had an insatiable appetite for sadism, Colton had no desire to see the scenario pan out; he could hazard a guess at the outcome without witnessing it first-hand.

Colton led Honey-Lou to another of the doors set into the playroom wall, and although a large part of him dreaded what grim delights they would find behind it, his curiosity was as aroused as his dick. Despite being party to the fate of the Greens, Colton found he was still as horny as hell and looking forward to enjoying Honey-Lou's inviting body. Colton's heart sank a little when he saw the clear plastic sheeting on the floor. That and the young woman suspended from the ceiling, legs spread wide, by her ankles; her wrists were tied together and secured to a thick metal hoop embedded in the floor. She was naked, of course, and her dark skin was shiny with sweat and the vivid pink of her exposed cunt contrasted wonderfully against her ebony skin. The woman was motionless, save for the laboured breathing that made her bee-sting tits rise and fall, and her darting, terrified eyes. Colton couldn't help but wonder what her crime had been to deserve this humiliation, or was she just the entertainment?

Beneath the woman, two couples lay entwined, the guys propped up on their elbows watching the girls making out.

"Welcome." One of the guys greeted Colton and Honey-Lou. "Thank you for joining us." Honey-Lou led

Colton toward the couples, wet and eager to join in with the fun.

"You are just in time for the main event," the other guy told them. As he struggled to his feet, his bulbous belly wobbled with a bizarre liquid motion, and for a moment, Colton thought that the guy would plop right back down again. But no, the fat guy managed to stay upright, his meagre stub of a penis pointing at the new arrivals.

Honey-Lou pulled on Colton's hand, maneuvering him toward the two women who were exploring each other's vulvas with frantic hands. She knelt down beside them, and one of the ladies held out a hand, wet and slippery from her lover's vagina, to welcome Honey-Lou into their tryst. Honey-Lou let go of Colton's hand and allowed herself to be drawn into the middle of the two women, to become one with their naked flesh; caressing their writhing bodies and joining her tongue with theirs in sensual, probing kisses.

The fat guy picked up a knife from a low table in the corner of the room and approached the suspended woman. The knife was a thin, double-edged blade with a polished wood handle, the type Colton had used as a boy on his frequent fishing trips with his father to prepare their catch for cooking.

"Would you like to—?" the fat guy asked Colton.

"Er, no," Colton replied. "Thank you, though." He offered a weak smile.

Fat guy slipped the knife into the suspended woman's cunt, and she attempted to struggle against her bonds. She screamed her surprise as the knife penetrated her most sensitive part and wriggled in a vain attempt to escape the searing pain.

As Colton watched, and Honey-Lou located a willing pussy to lap at, blood began to trickle from the woman's vagina and created a thin rivulet of crimson that made its way down along her belly and on toward her breasts.

"No. Please," she gasped, her eyes burning into Colton's.

Don't let this happen to me.

The fat guy pulled on the knife and slit his victim's body until the blade jarred to a halt at her sternum.

The woman let out a wet, shrill scream and thrashed against the ropes like a snared animal. Blood gushed out of her in a viscous flood as the slit in her belly gaped open, and the woman's innards slopped out.

Honey-Lou and her newly acquainted lesbian friends looked up from their endeavours as the dark-skinned woman's blood splashed over their bodies. The fat guy's friend stroked the three women, his chubby hands smearing the blood over their skin as an artist would paint on a canvass. And Colton noted he took particular delight with Honey-Lou's smooth pate.

The suspended woman gurgled and cried out as she choked on the pink coils of her own intestines and fought hopelessly against the stinking fluids from her ruptured bowel that poured up her nose.

Colton stood motionless, more than a little disturbed by what he was seeing. There was no getting away from the fact that, since this was his dream, it was his own troubled brain creating this nauseating spectacle. He couldn't help but gag at the stench of the woman's viscera, and he grew sickened at the sight of her struggles that grew weaker by the second. And at that point, Colton wanted nothing more than to be awake and away from all of this.

But then, before he knew what was happening to him, Honey-Lou had clawed his pants down to his ankles and was slurping noisily at his dick. She drew its length deep into her mouth and circled its swollen head with her expert tongue. She looked up at Colton, her face spattered with blood, her body a swirl of smeared red, and he found it difficult to read her expression, what with her lack of eyebrows and all; but Colton figured that she was having a good time.

And then Colton Forshay—at long last—fucked Honey-Lou Woolston. He lay her down on top of the two women and fucked her long and hard while Fat Guy sodomized his friend, and the freshly gutted woman died choking on her own guts.

*****

Colton and Honey-Lou only just managed to get cleaned up and presentable in time for Zack's briefing in conference room four. Their assigned living quarters each had a hot shower and a selection of fresh clothing. Colton had opted for jeans and a plain, short-sleeved shirt he thought made him look like Larry the Cable Guy, and Honey-Lou had went with a vivid pink mini dress that showed off her trim legs to perfection and scooped low at the front to display her bra-less tits.

"I'd like to begin by thanking all of you for attending this meeting." Zack sounded full of importance—mainly his own, Colton mused. Zack was on his feet at the head of the long boardroom table. It was obvious he was as high up in the rankings of the Resistance as was possible, and there was no real need for him to thank everyone; he'd made it damned clear it was required attendance.

Colton looked around, aside from himself, there was Honey-Lou, Eric, and Kunah; it looked to Colton like they were there to repay their debt for their rescue. On the opposite side of the polished, mahogany table sat half of a dozen of the ubiquitous Resistance fighters, not a smile between them. They all stared at Colton and his accidental cohorts with something akin to derision, although a couple of them appeared particularly mesmerized by the way Honey-Lou's unfettered nipples jutted against the flimsy material of her dress. Colton also noted that each of the foot soldiers were armed with mean-looking semi-automatics, which they had slung casually across their backs.

"The Big Plan." Zack got their attention. "We execute it tonight." The Resistance fighters nodded sagely; a little too keen to get to work with those guns for Colton's comfort. "President Ocelot is hosting a Devil's Roulette Ball this evening at the presidential palace, and whilst we know security will be stepped up, it does give us a rare opportunity to gain access—providing we have the right paperwork."

Colton studied Zack, struggling to reconcile that this dream-character who sounded so in control—so *commanding*—was essentially the same up-his-own-ass shrink that Zeenah now insisted he spill his guts to once a week.

"Devil's Roulette?" Colton asked, feeling as if he really should know the answer as everyone around the table looked at him as if he were some special kind of idiot.

"You have been out of circulation, haven't you?" Zack said with a smirk. A chuckle went around the table, and Honey-Lou patted Colton's knee as a show of support.

"I guess I have," Colton replied as his face reddened.

"For the uninitiated amongst us." Zack smiled. "And I guess that's just you, Colton." The leader of the Resistance seemed to relish his opportunity to make Colton feel small. "The Devil's Roulette is a sex game in which the participants are injected with a drug that will make them ejaculate blood until they bleed to death—once in the next six times they fuck following said injection."

Colton looked astounded. How come he knew nothing about this? This was supposed to be *his* dream, dammit!

"It may be the first time; it may be the sixth," Zack continued. "They say the thrill is in not knowing, and in taking the ultimate risk. Once the drug wears off—in twelve hours or so—it's all back to normal."

"I heard that the orgasms are just mind-blowing," Honey-Lou purred in Colton's ear. Her hand slid upward on his thigh, and her fingers brushed against his penis which was still a little sensitive and tender from their earlier tryst. With her other hand, much to the delight of Zack's soldiers, she absently twiddled with her nipple loops through her dress.

"That's the payoff," Zack added. "The most intense, brain-shredding sex you ever had in your life, for the chance that you might just bleed to death having it."

"Still, what a fucking good way to go, eh?" Eric chimed in, much to everyone's amusement.

Zack went on to explain the objective of the Big Plan was for the Resistance—himself, the soldiers, Colton, and his crew—to infiltrate the presidential palace during the debauched Devil's Roulette Ball shenanigans and kidnap President Ocelot. Simple as that. They were then to return the president to the Resistance headquarters, after which Zack's plan became a little nebulous.

"It's a dangerous mission," Zack affirmed. "Our most dangerous one yet, and not all of you will come back alive." He attempted a reassuring smile. "But, once we get our hands on the president, we will be able to find out why he is persecuting those who have the dream and put a stop to it.

"How, exactly, do you intend to do that?" Kunah asked, puzzled.

"We have our means," Zack replied.

Colton could see Zack was avoiding the direct question. Either his methods of truth extraction with telepathic ocelots were top secret, or he had no idea what he was going to do once he had successfully kidnapped the president. Colton rather feared the latter.

And all the while Zack was spouting his grand plans, Honey-Lou stroked Colton's dick through his jeans and had succeeded in stirring it back to life despite having exhausted it less than half an hour ago.

"Why are you making us go?" Eric asked. "It's not like we have any training for this."

"You are going because I say you are going." Zack's eyes narrowed and his voice lowered to a growl. "And because a bunch of regular folks will provide the perfect cover for the operation." He gave Eric a withering look.

Don't you dare ask any more questions, dog.

"We go at midnight; the president's shindig will be just getting started by then. Meantime, you will all be issued with guns."

Colton struggled to his feet, a more difficult task than it should have been, because of the throbbing erection—and Honey-Lou's nimble fingers—in his pants. He had to get out; out of this room *and* this dumb dream. Things had stopped being exciting and arousing and were getting out of hand now.

Since the prison, this whole thing had rapidly ceased being fun for Colton. The sexy stuff was one thing, and although he thoroughly enjoyed all of that, in its many guises and perversions, the violence he'd witnessed since arriving at the Resistance HQ had effectively counteracted that. He was even getting to be relatively comfortable with Zachary Stackhouse's intrusion into the dream, but the increasing propensity for brutality in this world he had created was beginning to weigh heavily on his sensitivities.

And now, now he was expected to go on some suicide mission with a gaggle of no-hopers and gung-ho soldiers? Hadn't he read somewhere that if you died in your dream, you died in real life? Not a chance Colton was willing to take.

Colton made his way out of the briefing room. If any of those inside cared that he was walking out, none of them showed it. Probably thought he was just going for a pee or to relieve the monster erection that he was sporting.

Once he got to the safe haven of the hallway, Colton leaned against the wall and closed his eyes. There was only one way out of this, and that was to wake the fuck up. So, Colton concentrated on just that and pinched hard on the soft skin on the underside of his wrist.

***

Colton awoke to find himself back on the park bench. The sun was bloated and orange on the horizon and stained the evening sky a rich pinkish orange. He felt a little ashamed he'd slept the day away like some common itinerant, slumped on the rough wooden park seat surrounded by pigeon crap.

At least, Colton consoled himself, he'd gotten away from the dream that had turned incredibly unpleasant very quickly. Sure, he'd enjoyed dreaming about ploughing the delectable Honey-Lou Woolston in the sensual surroundings of the Resistance building, even despite the eviscerations and murder that had gone on around him. That much was evident by the cold, drying crust of semen that soaked through his pants, making him feel uncomfortable. Colton sighed, part of him was delighted to be awake and back in the real world, but there was the other part that was disappointed at having to face that real world knowing his next task was to go home and explain to Zeenah he'd lost yet another job.

"Give me your wallet," a voice growled.

Colton jumped, and the skin prickled on the nape of his neck. He looked around. A burly looking youth stepped out from behind a bush, brandishing nothing more than the most enormous fists Colton thought he'd ever seen.

"Pardon me?" Colton stammered.

"I said, give me your fucking wallet," the youth reiterated. He placed a menacing emphasis upon *fucking*, which came out sounding a lot like *foookin'*.

"I-I don't have any money."

"I'll be the judge of what you have, or haven't got," the youth snarled and closed the gap between himself and Colton's bench. "Now, don't make me have to ask you again." The youth glanced around, sizing up the shadow-filled park for witnesses. Colton looked around too, hoping against hope that someone would jump to his defense here. Sadly, the only other soul aside from himself and his mugger was the old homeless lady who was still in the spot on the bench opposite and who was quite possibly dead.

Colton stood up and discovered the peculiar sensation of his legs being stiff and wobbly all at the same time. He held out his hands in a supplicant gesture.

"I really don't have any—"

The mugger launched himself at Colton, fists flailing, his face set in an ugly grimace. The first punch caught Colton square on the nose and the sickening *crunch* of breaking cartilage resounded through Colton's skull and thick, coppery blood poured down his throat. Colton staggered backward, and the back of his knees hit the bench. He went down with a dull smack on the park's asphalt path. He raised his hands above his head to fend off the youth's blows, but somehow those humongous fists kept on getting through.

Colton cried out for help, for mercy, for anything that would stop this frenzied assault on his person. As the assault progressed, Colton's cries were reduced to faint gurgles through the blood and snot that clogged up his mouth and nose.

The youth, soon tired of bending over to vent his rage at his victim, proceeded to kick at Colton as if he were an oversized soccer ball. Colton writhed around on the ground as each kick sent sharp flashes of pain through his body and added to his agony as he felt organs rupture and bones crack.

"Please! Stop!" Colton cried out in desperation. He could feel his brain beginning to cloud over as the sheer volume of pain signals running along his nerves overloaded his system. "Please!" Colton summoned a last ounce or two of strength from somewhere and struggled to try to get himself up from the ground. He managed to raise himself up on one broken arm, his cracked teeth gritted against the pain that flared up to his shoulder and the mugger paused. Colton felt what may have been a thin sliver of hope that he might just get out of this situation alive after all.

Then, one well-aimed kick connected with Colton's head; he saw a myriad of stars, and his vision turned a cloudy red as his eyes filled with blood. He felt the world float serenely away from him, and he dropped back down to the path. Colton's head connected hard with the ground, and he heard the sound from the inside of his own skull.

Thonk. And then all went black for Colton Forshay.

CHAPTER EIGHT

The bouncing of the SUV jolted Colton awake, and it took him a second or two to realize where he was.

"Must have had a good night, sleepy head?" he heard Eric say. "Looks like you tired yourselves out." Colton could hear the smirk in his dog/son's voice loud and clear. He looked up and saw that Honey-Lou was fast asleep too; her body slumped in her seat, head rattling gently on the car's window.

Colton felt a surge of panic spread through his body like somebody was injecting pure fear into his veins. He looked around; saw the other familiar faces of Kunah, their driver, and Zack. Through the rear window, a minivan that contained the half a dozen Resistance fighters, and—no doubt—their evil-looking guns, followed them.

Colton then realized he, too, was nursing a gun, as were the others in his vehicle. A little overkill for people who were only supposed to be infiltration cover, he thought. With that thought, dread gripped Colton's balls like a stone-cold vice, his stomach knotted up and he felt like he was going to throw up. Colton fought against the nausea with his usual technique and pinched hard at the soft side of his arm to wake himself up.

***

Zeenah Forshay gazed down at her husband's broken body as it lay motionless in the hospital bed. It broke her heart to see him like this. His face was swollen and bloodied and barely recognizable, his arms and legs were in casts, and there was a thick bandage around his shaved head. They'd taped his eyes shut, although that hardly seemed necessary to Zeenah given they were practically swollen shut by themselves, but the doctors had informed her it *was* necessary to prevent his eyes from drying out.

Myriad medical machines glowed and beeped in the ICU room and clear tubes snaked out from every one of Colton's orifices—along with some from holes the doctors had made in him especially for the purpose. Even Colton's breathing was made possible by a corrugated tube that invaded his mouth.

They'd told her Colton was in a deep, deep coma. That had been mostly down to the extensive head trauma he'd received in the attack. They weren't sure if the bleeding inside his skull had stopped completely, or how much of his delicate brain tissue had died. He may, the handsome young doctor had told her, never actually wake up and had she considered organ donation?

"I'm sure he'll be okay," a welcome voice soothed Zeenah. "He's a tough old bastard." An arm slipped around her trim waist.

"I hope so," Zeenah sighed. "I'd feel so bad if anything happened—"

She was silenced by a tender kiss. Zeenah reached for the soft lips with her tongue and pressed herself tight into her lover's body.

He pulled away.

"We can't," Dr. Zachary Stackhouse told her. "Not here."

***

"We're here," Zack announced as he brought the SUV to a halt in the crowded parking lot.

Colton peered out into the night and up at the imposing majesty of the presidential palace. The palace was built of light sandstone in a mock Gothic style that was complete with narrow arched windows and thick wooden doors studded with metal bolts for decoration. Colton craned his neck to see the top of the twin turrets that stood sentry on either side of the enormous facade, but found he couldn't see all the way up there, such was the sheer size of the place.

A smartly dressed valet waved the SUV through, and Zack gave him a friendly nod.

"We leave the guns in here for now," Zack told the others. "We are supposed to be here as guests, and the last thing we need is to arouse suspicion with these things." He patted his semi-automatic.

"Perhaps you should have given us smaller guns," Eric stated the obvious. Everyone agreed—much to Zack's chagrin—that, yes, that would have been a preferable idea.

"Team Two will enter the palace at oh-one-hundred hours," Zack made with his military speak. The soldiers in the minivan behind them had driven on to rear of the palace, where they would masquerade as security guards until go-time.

Zack climbed out of the SUV and handed the keys to the smiling valet. Colton hid his gun beneath his seat and followed suit, along with Eric, Honey-Lou, and Kunah. Kunah had the hardest time saying goodbye to his gun, having fallen hopelessly in love with it along the way; he planted a small, tender kiss on its barrel before secreting it under his seat.

"I always wanted to visit the palace," Honey-Lou said with her voice full of awe. She adjusted her dress upwards to cover the hint of dark pink areola that was making an escape, and pulled the hem down at the back to conceal at least some of the curve of her ass the valet was openly staring at.

As the valet drove the SUV away, Zack led the way up the stone steps to the palace, weaving his way between the other latecomers as if he were in a race to the door. Colton studied the other guests with a paranoid eye—what if even one of them had an inkling of his purpose here?

They soon reached the wide, oak door, and it swung open to welcome them into a spacious, marble-floored vestibule. Guarding either side of the doorway was a duo of women, both deliciously naked apart from the hefty guns they had slung over their shoulders. Colton saw, to his utter delight, they were identical twins; a perfect mirror image of one another down to the size and curve of their breasts and the color of the miniscule wisp of pubic hair that curled from between their muscular thighs. One of the guards stepped forward to prevent Zack's progress, her hand stroked the cool metal of her gun, and she smiled at him.

A third lady stepped forward—and to add to Colton's delight, he saw that they were triplets—clad in a houndstooth skirt suit that clung to each and every one of her curves like a second skin. She carried in her slender hand something that resembled those unconvincing ray guns that featured in low-budget 1970's space movies. She waved the would-be ray gun at Zack and his companions.

Zack rolled up his sleeve, and she pressed the gun to his arm.

Colton began to feel *really* scared and worried his guilt would show all over his face, which had suddenly felt warm and uncomfortable. He heard the *shhhhttt* sound that the gun made against Zack's arm and suddenly things were starting to get far too real, and he had a feeling that he wouldn't be able to wake up from this.

"Sleeve," one of the guards purred at Colton. She fondled her gun's clip as if it were a lover's penis, a half smile on her lips.

Colton did as he was ordered—how could he not? The suited lady pressed the cold metal of the gun to his arm. Again, Colton heard the sound it made, and he felt a cold pressure on his arm as something chilled was injected through his skin and then he was done.

"You are now participants in the Devil's Roulette," Suit-lady smiled at Colton. "Enjoy."

Eric went next, followed by Kunah, then the five were ushered toward a door at the end of the vestibule. As they reached that door, which was a little narrower than the main door but no less imposing, Colton began to experience a strong feeling of *déjà vu*. It seemed to him that whichever architect had designed the office building that now housed Resistance HQ had plagiarized a lot of their ideas from the presidential palace.

The door burst open, and Colton had to jump back to avoid being hit. He instinctively pulled Eric and Honey-Lou out of the way, and in doing so, most likely saved them from serious injury. Two paramedics exited the door, followed by the overpowering waft of incense, pheromones, and sex sweat from the room beyond. They maneuvered a stretcher through the doorway upon which writhed a broad-shouldered guy with bleach-blond hair. The guy was covered with a white sheet, but was obviously naked beneath, and the sheet itself was rapidly turning into a sopping wet crimson mess.

Colton, Eric, and Honey-Lou stared at the guy on the stretcher as the paramedics took him by. The guy let out a yowl that somehow managed to sound agonized and orgasmic at the same time. His body arched, and he ejaculated another jet of blood into the sheet. Colton cringed and stroked at the spot on his arm where the lady in the suit had injected him with *something*.

"You need to be careful, guys," Zack told Colton, Eric, and Kunah as the paramedics took the guy outside. "That could easily be any of us now they've injected that shit into us." They heard the patient scream out once more, then the door thumped closed and he was gone. "Remember, it could be the first time, it could be the sixth." Zack put on his serious face and raised his arm to illustrate his point. Colton could see the faintest trace of a red mark on Zack's arm where he'd been given his shot. "We all have the Devil's Roulette drug inside of us now, so I'd say we would be best served focusing on finding the president and meeting our objective; better to abstain."

Easier said than done, Colton thought to himself. The door to the inner sanctum opened once more, and he was confronted with the orgiastic atmosphere, wall-to-wall gorgeous people and wanton displays of debauchery that made the O'Keefes' barbecue look like a Sunday school outing.

They stepped through the door and into a vast ballroom filled with beautiful people as far as the eye could see. Some were dressed in the most revealing of outfits, some in exquisitely expensive lingerie, others preferred to be entirely naked. The ballroom's ceiling was high and vaulted—a far grander version than that of the Resistance headquarters—and was painted with exquisitely explicit scenes of entwined, fornicating nudes. The windowless walls were clad in smooth, shiny black Italian marble from floor to ceiling, and at the end, farthest away from the door, a huge, polished granite staircase swept upward to the second-floor balcony. And beyond that balcony lay the president's private quarters. As befitting its status, the staircase was guarded by two familiar looking naked guards.

They were quintuplets? Or had President Ocelot finally perfected human cloning?

There was a string quartet in one corner of the room to provide atmospheric music as a background to the sex and licentiousness going on; the musicians—two guys, two girls—were naked, and their slender bodies had been painted with musical notes with each having a meandering row of piano keys painted along their thighs.

Everywhere Colton looked as he followed Zack and Honey-Lou through the throng, people were in the pre-amble to, or in the throes of sex. Each and every possible permutation of gender and multiples of participants was on wanton display. There was no orifice unexplored, no fetish disallowed, no taboos at all. The guests all laughed and talked, kissed and caressed, stroked and fingered, sucked and fucked; all the while plucking exotic cocktails from the trays carried by the ever-present lingerie-clad wait staff.

Unlike in the Resistance building, this place was just one big playroom with no side rooms for even a modicum of privacy. Everyone here indulged in their chosen debauchery for the entertainment of everyone else; there were no secrets at the presidential palace.

"This is *so* awesome." Honey-Lou grinned at Colton like a cat that caught the mouse as she stepped carefully over a young couple who were busy fucking on the floor. "I've heard all the stories about this place and its wild parties," she said. "But wow." Her eyes burned into Colton's, and her erect nipples betrayed her arousal.

She gripped Colton's hand and led him on through the crowd, so distracted she was only half-heartedly following Zack. She nimbly steered Colton around a foursome who were all dressed head to toe in black PVC catsuits that made each one of them seem somehow asexual. They stood in the center of the ballroom, oblivious to everything around them, groping and licking each other through the thick plastic, and Colton wondered what they were possibly getting out of the experience.

Eric and Kunah trailed behind Colton, Honey-Lou, and Zack. Zack made his way purposefully toward the staircase, incredibly single-minded and oblivious to the sights, sounds, and smells of sex in its every perversion that surrounded him.

They made their way past a St. Andrew's cross upon which was tied a bronzed muscular young man. He was strapped to the wooden cross face inward and three young ladies were taking it in turns to fist his ass, impervious to his cries to be set free and the blood that ran down his legs. Dodging between the guy on the cross and one of his tormentors who was wielding a large tube of lubricant and a latex glove, Colton tripped over a pairing of girls. Both were redheads, their hair tied into ponytails so severe it stretched the skin on their faces taut and distorted their eyes to give them a distinctly oriental appearance. They were knelt on all fours on the ballroom floor, butt facing butt, impaled on either end of an impossibly thick, glass dildo. They fucked each other at a frantic pace, groaning and screaming in ecstasy, not pausing for a second when Colton all but fell on top of them.

Honey-Lou stared at the girls with a hungry lust in her eyes. One of them reached up to her and slid a hand along the inside of Honey-Lou's thighs. Honey-Lou gasped as a probing finger slipped inside her pussy, and then moaned out loud as it began to wriggle around in the warm and wet to pull her toward the lesbian tryst.

Colton watched with interest as Honey-Lou was drawn into the girl's scene by her cunt. He grinned and squeezed his cock as she took no time at all in pressing her face between the two pairs of sweat-sheened buttocks to lick at the transparent dildo as it slid in and out of the two girls, all the while groping at the fat, hanging breasts on offer. Colton stroked Honey-Lou's smooth head and figured that he would leave her to her indulgences for now, and he fought the urge to kneel himself down and fuck her from behind there and then.

Zack had paused at the periphery of a group of twelve or so people. Colton and Eric caught up with him - Kunah had wandered off by then—and eased themselves into the group in their effort to not stick out like a bunch of Resistance fighters there to kidnap the president.

In the center of the small but growing crowd, a guy lay on his back and he was straddled by two large-breasted women. The women, one with skin as dark as the finest molasses, the other a golden tan, had his dick sandwiched between their tits. As they massaged his penis, they took it in turns to spit onto their cleavage as a means of lubrication and with each gob of saliva, the guy let out a loud groan.

"This is his fifth fuck; he's really pushing his luck now." Colton heard someone whisper, and he realized why there was a crowd around what was, by comparison, a tame scene. They were there for the same reason people flocked to watch Evel Knievel jump two dozen school busses.

To watch the crazy bastard fall.

The guy's groans became louder and more frequent as his writhing beneath the weight of the women's bodies increased. He thrust his dick with jerking pelvic motions into the soft, liquid tissue of their breasts, encouraged by the soft moans of the women who squeezed their tits tight together around his slippery cock.

And then he came. With an ear-piercing shriek, the man bucked so fiercely he threw the dark-skinned woman clear off leaving her partner in crime with his penis pumping its thick blood between her tits.

The gathering gasped and took a collective step back, all enjoying the spectacle but unwilling to be sprayed with the man's gruesome ejaculate. A ripple of applause went around the spectators as the man squirted his life's blood between the girl's breasts, and he began to experience the biggest post-coital regret of his life.

The dark-skinned woman helped up her friend, who was by now drenched top to bottom in slick blood, and led her away. In their wake came the paramedics with their stretcher and half of a dozen dwarves dressed in nothing but miniature rubber butcher's aprons.

As the paramedics carted the poor guy away, his cries pitifully muted, and his ejaculations weakening, the dwarves began to mop up the blood with paper towels and tiny mops. In an incredibly short space of time, it looked as if nothing had ever happened in that particular spot of the ballroom.

Colton once again found himself to be uncomfortably turned on; the erection that pressed against his pants for escape was quite painful. Although he had just witnessed firsthand the Devil's Roulette in action, his libido was already beginning to take over his common sense. And the more he looked around at the naked displays of raw animal sex and perversion, the more he ached to plunge his dick into something—*anything*—and to hell with the consequences.

***

Kunah found himself distracted by a petite girl with raven-black hair and the darkest of brown eyes. She looked most spectacular in her purple satin bustier that hiked up and accentuated her breasts to overflowing, which she complemented with spiked stiletto mini boots and a black leather strap-on harness.

Naturally, it was the harness that attracted Kunah. He couldn't help but admire the way it clung to her tiny waist, and the broad straps that ran around her back and down beneath her pear-shaped ass; and just how was he supposed to resist those polished brass buckles that held the whole ensemble together? All Kunah wanted to do was to make hot sweet love to that harness.

So, he forgot about the others, about the mission, and followed the girl of his deepest desires around the ballroom. Before long, inevitably, she confronted him.

"Are you stalking me?" she demanded to know.

"Err, no, I mean, possibly, I mean—I'm sorry," Kunah stammered, not once being able to take his eyes off of the harness that looked even more appetizing to him from the front. He allowed his eyes to feast on the circle of black leather over her pussy, to study the detail of how exquisitely it dug into the soft folds of her plump lips. The leather there was impregnated with tiny brass studs, into which a phallus could be inserted, and he imagined his dick sliding deep inside.

"You want to touch it?" the girl asked, already seeing the answer in the objectophile's eyes.

"Yes. Please." Kunah reached out a trembling hand and touched his fingertips to the leather straps, and he shuddered with sheer delight.

"I think you and I could have a lot of fun together." The girl smiled. "Come with me." And so saying, she gripped his hand and led him through the crowd toward the staircase. "Not just anyone is allowed up here," the girl told Kunah as they approached the security women at the foot of the stairs. "But a true objectophile, now that's something the president will make an exception for."

"Me? How did you know?" Kunah asked, reaching out to touch the harness again.

"Takes one to know one, I guess." The girl laughed, and her eyes shone with a delightful wickedness.

Kunah followed the girl up the stairs, his eyes transfixed on her tight behind and those sensual straps. Oh, the things he could do with those delicious straps; Kunah's dick twitched just thinking about it.

From the top of the stairs, the view from the balcony was breathtaking. The ever-moving sea of naked and almost-naked bodies milled around: some indulging, some watching, most touching or tasting. Small groups formed and unformed and re-formed within the throng, each absorbed in their own fantasies and exploring everyone and everything around them. Everyone down there was oblivious to observers and those playing around them. And the men, they seemed impervious to the deathly gamble they were taking with their lives in the name of sexual fulfilment.

From the balcony, the corseted girl led Kunah into one of the many side rooms. It was dark inside, the only illumination coming from a handful of fat church candles that flickered yellow flames and cast shadows over the twin bed that was the room's only furnishing. The bed itself was neatly made with a dark-red comforter and a single matching pillow.

The girl unhooked her bustier at the back and slid it off to completely reveal her breasts. She then undressed Kunah, hooked his fingers under the back strap of her harness, and led him to the bed.

Once on the bed, Kunah pressed his eager erection into the girl, ground it into the firm flesh of her ass as it sought out the harsh leather straps beneath the comforter.

"Take your time," she whispered. "I want to hold you first; I want to feel close to you." She flipped Kunah over and spooned him from behind.

Kunah lay still and enjoyed the feel of the girl's skin pressed onto his and the way it made him tingle all over. He closed his eyes; he could feel the jutting nipples that dug into his back and the soft skin of her flat stomach as it rose and fell as she breathed her warm breath onto the nape of his neck.

He felt her move and then grasp his penis. Kunah moaned with delight. It was time to enjoy that delicious harness.

Before Kunah could turn over in the bed to face the girl and take his pleasure from her and the harness, she had sliced off his penis with a straight razor she had kept hidden beneath the pillow.

Kunah felt only a slight tug on his dick as the blade ran across it, followed by the chill of cool air on the stump of his dick coupled with a sudden hot gush of blood on his legs. He tried to struggle free but the girl—and most likely the drugs he'd been given—held him in place, unable to cry out.

The girl slotted Kunah's severed cock into her harness and secured it tight by means of the leather loop. She dipped a hand between her own legs and used her own juices to wet Kunah's dick. And then, whilst the severed cock was still hard, and whilst Kunah Shah bled to death, the girl fucked him in the ass with his own dick.

The girl's breathing became heavy and labored as she ground into Kunah. She threw back the comforter to expose their perverse coupling to the room.

"This is what President Ocelot wants," the girl grunted in Kunah's ear as she sodomised him. "His mind is inside mine, and you are inside you. This is what pleases him."

Kunah had felt his own cock slide into his anus with ease; and he was forced to admit it felt good. Detached as he was from the reality of his own impending demise, he rocked his body in time to the girl's thrusts and delighting in the *full* feeling it gave him.

A door—hidden by the shadows and camouflaged to resemble the wall—creaked open and Kunah saw four figures enter. One was the unmistakable, diminutive feline shape and beautiful markings of President Ocelot; the others, two white-clad, vacant-looking women and an elderly man who seemed barely able to walk.

They stood awhile and watched but were gone before corset girl reached her own screeching climax, and Kunah Shah slipped quietly into death.

CHAPTER NINE

Somewhat disgusted by his own growing arousal, and eager to stave it off before he was tempted to fuck himself into an early grave, Colton decided to find Honey-Lou. Eric had long since bounded off to join in a watersports game in the corner behind the string quartet. Colton glanced over and saw his dog/son drenched with the piss of a half a dozen people, leg cocked against a crouching woman and peeing in her face as she laughed and tried to catch the yellow stream in her mouth. *He always could pee a lot*, thought Colton.

Colton spied Zack glancing at his watch and looking anxiously toward the staircase. He nodded at Colton and tapped his watch and Colton acknowledged him.

Almost time.

Honey-Lou was busy being banged by one of the redhaired women, her vagina stretched wide by the more than substantial glass dildo; through the clear sides of the dildo, Colton could see deep into the luscious pink walls of Honey-Lou's cunt. She had her head buried between the legs of the other redhead, tongue fucking whilst the woman slapped her shiny bald dome in paroxysms of orgasmic delight.

Colton was too polite to interrupt, so he waited for Honey-Lou to come up for air before letting her know he was there. Watching his friend's sweat-drenched body squirming between two hot women did nothing but fuel Colton's troublesome arousal, but he fought the urge to play the Devil's Roulette for himself and plunge his aching dick into any one of the willing holes on offer.

"Hey, Colton," Honey-Lou greeted him, her face slick and glistening with the faintest tinge of blood on her lips. "You want to join?"

"We need to go," Colton shook his head. "Zack."

Honey-Lou extracted herself from the pussy she'd been eating with an apology. Her muse looked a little disappointed but shrugged and began to masturbate. With great reluctance, Honey-Lou eased herself off the double-header which slid from her sopping cunt with a soggy *shlurp*. She gave the other redhead a lingering, wet kiss on the mouth.

"Thank you," she purred. "Sorry I have to go." She licked the woman's lips and then stood up to go. Before Colton and Honey-Lou had taken more than a few steps, the redheads were once more impaled on the double-dong and squealing in pleasure.

A commotion from above caught Colton's attention.

"They've got the president!" a shrill voice wailed. "Somebody help!" The owner of the voice—a black-haired girl who wore a strap-on harness and was covered in fresh blood—appeared at the top of the stairs. There was the sharp crackle of gunfire, and the girl's left breast exploded to leave a gaping hole in her chest and spatter the marble staircase with bloodied shreds of flesh. She crumpled lifelessly to the floor amidst a cacophony of horrified screams from the ballroom below.

Behind her appeared the president and his small entourage, flanked by six black-clad figures, each one pointing a gun at his presidential head.

The revellers below panicked as pleasures of the flesh quickly gave way to self-preservation. They ran toward the main doors, trampling over those not quick enough to get up off the floor and those who fell.

The armed guards at the foot of the staircase ran up the stairs, guns drawn, magnificently nude bodies belying their deadly intentions.

"Stop them!" the president shouted, his disembodied voice booming from the throat of the elderly man by his side.

Colton heard the president's shout above the hubbub of the partygoers. Moreover, he *felt* it inside his head. The president had screamed out his order with his renowned psychic power, and it made Colton's head ache like a rotted tooth.

More guards responded to the president's distress, appearing from hidden rooms along the balcony and battling their way against the fleeing crowd in the ballroom. Colton grabbed Honey-Lou's hand and pulled her to the side of the ballroom, where they pressed themselves tight against the wall. He looked across to see Eric doing much the same behind the now vacant bandstand. Colton spotted Zack across the ballroom. He was fighting his way, like a salmon upstream, toward the staircase; eyes were fixed firmly on the two guards who were closing in on his soldiers. A palace security guard appeared from a concealed door on the wall next to Zack. As she ran past Zack, her gun held high above the heads of the crowd, Zack pounded on her back with his fist. He brought her down with ease, and her head connected with the hardwood floor with a smack. Zack twisted the girl's head sharp around, and Colton could have sworn he heard her neck snap even above the din of terrified voices.

Zack tore the gun from the dead guard and pushed his way toward the staircase. The soldiers on the balcony looked scared. They had President Ocelot, his aide, and his pair of concubines at gunpoint. But the presidential guards—about a dozen of them—were closing in, and there were armed guards on the stairs. The Resistance fighters fought to maintain their composure and nudged their captives toward the stairs.

Zack reached the bottom of the staircase and accidentally stepped on a guy who was dressed in a soiled adult diaper and rubber pants. As Zack's weight went on the guy's torso, the rubber pants gave out, and the diaper's contents spilled out with an unmistakeable stink. Zack ignored the gross smell, aimed the purloined gun at the peachy backsides of the naked guards and fired.

Zack's stolen gun made short work of the guards. They barely had the time to cry out before they were ripped to shreds by the hail of bullets from below them. One of the girls was cut almost in half, and her innards spilled out as she collapsed and cascaded down the stairs; the other was transformed in an instant to a bloodied mess of mashed flesh, dead before she even hit the hard stairs. Zack then turned his attention to the remaining guards who were crouched behind the balustrades on the balcony. Whilst they were practically invisible to Zack's men opposite, they were an open target to Zack down in the ballroom.

Zack's men urged the president toward the stairs and began their descent.

"Kill them!" This time, the President's voice resounded even louder than before, received by everyone in the ballroom. The elderly man beside the president kept his mouth firmly closed, and he clapped his hands to his head as President Ocelot screamed out his telepathic order directly into the heads of his people.

The palace guards on the balcony opened fire, and three of Zack's soldiers went down in a misty spray of blood as bullets peppered them. The remaining three hunkered down behind the opposite gallery along with the president, his elderly aide, and the concubines. They traded shots with the presidential guards, taking four out before they too hunkered down.

There was gunfire from across the ballroom, aimed at Zack. Colton saw him duck and weave between the panicking people, using their naked bodies for cover. Focussed solely upon the safety of the president to the exclusion of all others, the guards now fired indiscriminately into the bolting crowd, not caring how many they made collateral damage. Mercifully, many of the Devil's Roulette revellers had made their way out of the ballroom; although, some had been crushed against the walls *near* to the door or died trampled underfoot and lay where they had fallen leaving naked, bleeding, twisted bodies with snapped bones in puddles of their own blood.

Still reeling from the president's telepathic assault on his brain, Colton edged his way, back pressed against the wall, toward the door. Honey-Lou gripped his hand so tight it hurt, but he gritted his teeth against the pain and pulled her along behind him. She sobbed quietly, horrified by the carnage, desperate to be away from it all.

"When I say run, run for the door," Colton said, ducking down as stray bullets zinged by his head. "Don't look back, just fucking run!"

Honey-Lou nodded and forced a weak smile, and Colton was forced to admit she still looked mighty fine in the tiny pink dress, especially as her tits had practically bounced free at the top amidst all of the panic, and the hem had ridden up to expose a tantalizing glimpse of the plump pussy lips Colton remembered with a dick-stiffening fondness.

There was increased gunfire as the guards reached the foot of the staircase and shot at Zack's men on the balcony above. Their bullets missed and did little more than chip holes in the expensive marble stairs. The Resistance fighters returned fire and because it was easier to shoot downhill than up, mowed down the president's guards like they were targets at a shooting range. They continued their descent, poking the president with their guns to incentivize his cooperation.

Colton looked around; he'd lost track of Zack, so he kept his focus firmly on his escape route. The main door to the ballroom was almost clear now. The revellers who were not already dead or dying had gotten themselves out and were, by now, outside and running for their dear lives.

Almost there.

"Run!" Colton wriggled his hand free from Honey-Lou's grip and pushed her toward the door. He watched her run with her bare feet slap-slapping on the floor as she weaved her way through the litter of bodies strewn across the ballroom floor. Colton took a deep breath and ran after her.

The sharp retort of fresh gunfire split the air, and Colton saw two presidential guards appear from the secret door. Their voices were set to scream mode and their guns a-blazing. A shrill, pained scream from the stairs distracted Colton's attention, and he glanced away from Honey-Lou's butt and up toward the stairs. Two of the three Resistance soldiers had taken bullets—one to the head, one to the chest—and they lay slumped and lifeless on the stairs. The president's elderly aid clutched at his stomach, trying to stem the flood of crimson that bubbled from the gaping wound there, and one of the president's concubines was limp and bump-bumping down the remainder of the stairs. As she fell, her skull made a wet cracking noise on each stair, and Colton could plainly see the ugly lump at the back of her neck where the spine was broken. The other concubine—the one who had screamed out—well, that white-robed beauty with the blank, emotionless face—

"*Alicia,*" Colton's lips barely moved as he uttered his wife's name.

Colton stopped dead in his tracks, transfixed by the sight of the love he had thought was dead. She looked as beautiful now as she did the last time he had seen her alive, although her nose did appear just a tad bent out of place. Her body, barely hidden beneath the flimsy white robe, had maintained its magnificence, and her hair was as golden and fine as ever. But her eyes —those beautiful, wide eyes that had so entranced Colton—seemed dead and stared straight ahead as she stood beside her president on the stairs.

Behind Colton, another security guard ran towards the stairs. She flicked off her gun's safety and made ready to fire at the last remaining Resistance fighter, oblivious to Colton's presence directly in front of her. Aware of the movement, Colton spun around too late to get out of the way, still too shell-shocked to hit the ground.

Another blurred movement, and the guard fired.

Colton found himself on the hard floor of the ballroom, Eric on top of him as bullets whizzed over his head and on to their target.

"You nearly got yourself killed," Eric growled with a smile.

"Alicia," was all Colton could manage to say.

Eric leapt up from Colton's prone body and launched himself at the security guard as she ran by. He knocked her sprawling to the floor and forced the wind out of her lungs. Before she could take another breath, Eric had her throat in his jaws and was shaking her like a trapped rabbit.

Stunned by Eric's uncharacteristic display of blood lust, Colton could only watch in disbelief as his dog/son tore the struggling guard's throat from her neck and swallowed the bloodied gobbet of flesh whole.

More gunfire and the remaining two security guards died where they stood. Zack appeared through the secret door, dressed as a presidential guard. The uniform he had on had a small, round, bloody hole in the chest that looked fresh, and Colton didn't have to guess twice how Zack had come by it.

Zack ran to the president.

"Come with me, Sir," he said to the terrified cat. "We need to get you to safety."

President Ocelot complied, taking Zack on face value. His concubine—Colton's Alicia—and his wounded aide followed on.

Zack led them to the secret door, followed by a bewildered Colton and the bloodied Eric, and soon they were out of the ballroom and into the safety of the dark, narrow tunnel. As the door eased shut behind them, and they left behind the acrid stink of cordite, blood, and spilled guts, Colton heard the panicked voices of more guards as they arrived at the ballroom.

"Where did they go?"

"What happened to the president?"

"It must be the Resistance."

Zack led the way along the tunnel; the president appeared happy the man leading him to safety was a presidential guard. Just who the hell he thought Colton and Eric were, Colton didn't care to imagine. The remains of the president's entourage stumbled along behind; Colton found himself with Alicia for the first time in two years, and he was lost for words.

Colton studied his wife from behind, taking in the wonderful familiarity of her hourglass figure with its firm, round rump and tiny waist and the sensual way in which her hips swayed when she walked on those dainty feet of hers.

But he had sat there and watched her die.

That may be, thought Colton, *but this is my damn dream and for once it's going my way.*

***

Zack pushed open the door at the end of the tunnel, and they were greeted by a rush of cool night air. Colton could see the parking lot over to his left and figured they had come out of the palace somewhere along its right-hand side.

"This way, Sir." Zack kept up the pretence with President Ocelot. "There's a car waiting."

He led the ragtag group to the front of the palace where countless guards marched around pointing guns in a menacing yet desperate way at the last of the party guests, most of whom just seemed to be in shock and wandering around aimlessly. The guards had also set up a block across the driveway; it was a flimsy wooden barrier that rose up in the air to allow only scrutinised people to leave.

Colton felt that all too familiar fear creep into his guts as they neared a group of guards, convinced they would rumble Zack's flimsy plan.

The SUV appeared, and the smiling valet climbed out and handed Zack the keys.

"The girl's inside." The valet twitched his head to indicate Honey-Lou who was riding shotgun. "Kunah?"

"He's on his own," Zack said without feeling. "Or dead."

"See you back at headquarters."

Zack nodded an acknowledgement to the faux valet and ushered everyone into the black vehicle. Colton climbed in after Alicia to make sure he could sit next to her; he hoped he would find something to say.

"What is this?" the president asked through his aide's mouth. "Where are you taking me?" the president's aide said, his voice strained through his pain.

"Somewhere safe, Sir," Zack said and a worried look flashed across his face; this was the part where his play acting fell apart.

"This is not protocol." The aide was actually coughing up blood now, but still the president persisted through him.

"It is now, you fucking furball," Zack snarled and stamped on the gas pedal.

The SUV roared away, sending presidential guards and party guests alike scattering out of the way. There were shouts of "*halt!*" which Zack dutifully ignored as he raced on toward the barrier.

Colton heard the screech of wheels behind them and looked back to see a black minivan with heavily tinted windows set off after them. It ploughed into the valet who was too busy watching the SUV's dash for freedom. The unfortunate guy screamed as he bounced up onto the windshield, up over the roof, and fell silent when he smashed back down onto the concrete driveway; Colton turned away as the pretend valet's head burst like a kid's water balloon.

Zack crashed the SUV through the guard's barrier and splinters of red-striped wood showered down on the shocked guards. They fired at the retreating SUV, only to watch helplessly as their bullets bounced harmlessly from its bullet-proof exterior.

The minivan chased after the SUV, scattering people who got in the way and mowing down those who didn't move quickly enough as it roared down the driveway.

"Hold on, people!" Zack shouted and peeled the SUV out of the palace driveway and on to the road beyond.

The sudden change of direction threw Zack's passengers around in the SUV. The president's aide, who was still bleeding badly from his stomach, yelped in pain as Alicia fell on top of him and her elbow dug into his stomach wound, bringing forth another wash of blood. The president growled and cowered between the seats with nervous eyes on Honey-Lou and the gun she had pointed at his face. Eric had remained in his place, having been the only one in the back of the vehicle with the sense to put on his seat belt. He looked over at Colton with worried eyes.

Colton helped Alicia off the presidential aide and got her sitting upright again. The sleeve of her gown was soaked through with the aide's blood, but she seemed not to notice.

"Hey," Colton found a word to say to his wife. He stroked a strand of hair away from her face and looked into her eyes.

Nothing.

Those beautiful eyes, once so full of love and wicked promises, stared blankly back at Colton. If eyes were, as the poets mused, the windows to the soul, then his beloved Alicia's soul was dead.

She leaned forward and kissed him.

Alicia's lips were as plump and soft and warm as Colton's memory had preserved them, her tongue as moist and probing as ever. Yet somehow, there was something missing. It was as if she was there, but not *really* there, and it made as little sense as that to Colton. He pulled away from his wife's kiss to stare into her expressionless face and choked back a tear or two.

The SUV careened around a corner and onto a narrow, rough road. Colton held on to Alicia to stop her from falling onto the poor aide again and felt her body stiffen at his touch. The black minivan followed them no more than fifty yards behind and looked all the more sinister for not being able to see the occupants through the blackened windows. It was as if it was driving itself.

"They're gaining on us," Eric said, stating the fucking obvious.

"No shit." Honey-Lou smiled at him, her steady hand keeping that gun pointed at the trembling president.

Zack floored the pedal, and the SUV lurched onward. It kicked up loose scraps of the poorly maintained road and hurled them at the minivan on his tail. Closer and closer still, the minivan was almost within striking distance.

Colton had seen on police shows the technique they used to stop vehicles in instances such as this. They would simply hit the rear of the perpetrator's vehicle, and it would lose control and spin around a few times but would stop with its passengers intact. He was sure the guards wouldn't risk shooting at their president, but ramming the SUV certainly made some sense. Colton began to brace himself—physically as well as mentally—for the inevitable shunt. He cursed as his teeth rattled together, and he bit his tongue as the SUV ran over what felt like a cattle grid.

And then, suddenly, the minivan was gone.

Zack stomped on the brakes and brought the SUV to a screeching halt. He wound down his window, leaned out and waved. Four Resistance fighters stepped out from the bushes. They were dressed in black uniforms and carried the biggest guns Colton had seen thus far. They approached with caution to the gaping, rectangular hole in the road into which the presidential guards' minivan had fallen. Colton could hear shouts and thumping from inside the carefully planned ambush hole, which was the sound of the guards trying to get out.

It wasn't until the Resistance fighters sprayed into the hole with intense fire that Colton realized that the guns they were carrying were flame-throwers. The bulky tanks strapped to their backs should really have given it away, but hey, it was dark out there. The four guys backed into the bushes as the minivan caught alight, and Colton was sure he could hear the panicked, agonized screams of the guards inside as they began to roast.

Bon appetit.

The men closed the hole up by sliding a large steel plate over it. It effectively shut out the flames and smoke that could give away their position and sealed the guards into their burning fate. Zack drove away, and they all heard the dull *THWUMP* as the minivan's gas tank exploded in its underground tomb.

***

The rough country road soon turned into a dirt track filled with potholes which bounced the SUV around like a boat on rough seas. For Colton and the others, this made for a very uncomfortable half hour; none more so than the presidential aide who groaned at every jiggle of the vehicle and appeared to be fighting a losing battle to contain his abdominal contents. He slouched forward in his seat and clung tight to his stomach, as the pink, pulsing coils of his intestines slid through his fingers, a little more with each bump of the SUV.

After what felt like an eternity of peering through the windows and sunroof for signs of the presidential guard following them by road or air; of inhaling the stink of the dying aide's blood and bowel contents; of sitting next to the shell of his wife, Colton was grateful beyond words when Zack pulled up in front of a small cottage in the middle of a forest.

Zack killed the engine and switched off the lights. They all sat there in the darkness with an air of anticipation, staring at the lifeless cottage. There were no lights on, no curtains twitching and even the grass that grew in an unruly tangle around the small, wooden house seemed lackluster.

Suddenly, the outside light blazed on, and the cottage door opened. Out stepped a large, rather unconvincing transvestite. He was big, black, and broad and was wearing full makeup. He was dressed rather stylishly in a white pencil skirt/pink blouse ensemble, the latter of which had ruffles down the middle to enhance the cleavage.

"Ya comin' in or not?" the transvestite's voice boomed loud and crisp in the night.

"We're going in," Zack informed his passengers. He unbuckled his seatbelt, opened the door, and got out.

"Good to see ya," the transvestite greeted Zack. He stepped carefully on the uneven ground, progress made uncertain by the precipitous heels on his huge feet.

"You too, Chardonnay." Zack hugged his *compadre*. "You really are a sight for sore eyes."

"Same to ya, Zack." Chardonnay smiled, eyes twinkling with what may well have been a lover's shine. "Ya had me worried that ya'd not made it out of the palace."

"Nah, we did good," Zack told him. "Lost some good guys, though," he sighed.

"They knew the risks," Chardonnay comforted, "we all do." He play thumped Zack on the shoulder, almost knocking his leader over. "So, you have the goods?"

"Of course." Zack perked up. He motioned for the others in the SUV to join him. Colton helped the aide to climb out of the van. The poor old guy was bent over and cupping his guts with his withered old hands and groaned with every step. *Probably wise not to stand straight*, Colton thought. Alicia clambered from the vehicle with grace, followed by Eric who padded by her side, his face filled with curiosity. Honey-Lou escorted the reluctant President Ocelot from the SUV and pretty much dragged him most of the way to the cottage by the scruff of his neck.

"You will not get away with this, Dreamers," President Ocelot growled through his aide. The aide moaned loudly at the exertion of having to speak the president's words and leaned heavily against Eric to avoid collapse.

Chardonnay crouched down to face the president. He ruffled the silky fur between the Ocelot's ears and traced the intricate pattern on his coat with long, strong fingers.

"How do you *do* that?" Chardonnay asked. The president just glowered at him, his feline eyes narrowed to angry slits.

"We'd best get inside." Zack hurried everyone into the cottage, keen to have the outside light switched off and the concealing cover of night over their escapade.

The cottage was cozy inside, a euphemism for cramped. There was the main room, which also housed the kitchenette—a four-ring stove, oven, microwave, and a Belfast sink—off of which were two small bedrooms, complete with queen-sized beds. No TV, no radio, no books.

"If y'all want the pooper, it's out back," Chardonnay informed his guests. "And watch out for the black widows under the seat." He pronounced widows as *widders,* which made Colton wonder exactly what the guy in the skirt's accent was *supposed* to be.

"Must make a note to pick a safehouse with indoor plumbing next time," Zack said as a little of his good humor made a welcome return. "At least we can lay low here for a few hours 'til the heat dies down."

"You just kidnapped the president, Zack," Chardonnay reminded him. "I don't think the heat's gonna die down anytime soon."

"We have to get him back to HQ," Zack replied. "Find out what the fuck is going on with all this dream shit."

"You'll find out nothing," the president's aide sputtered through a mouthful of dark blood.

"Shouldn't we do something for him?" Honey-Lou asked.

"Nothing much we can do," Zack told her. "At least until we get back to headquarters."

"You don't have a first aid kit here?" Eric added.

"I do, honey," Chardonnay said. "But I think yo' man here needs more than a Band-Aid and a couple of Ibuprofen caps, don't you?"

Eric looked over at the old man with the ashen face who lay curled up on the floor in front of the three-bar fire and shook his head. The transvestite was right, of course; nothing much they could do to prevent the old boy's slow evisceration in the middle of the forest.

"I'm gonna get some rest," Zack announced. He made his way to one of the bedrooms and closed the door behind himself.

"I could do with some sleep, too," Colton said. "Is it okay if we take the other room?"

"Sure thing, hun," Chardonnay smiled. "Be my guest."

"I think I'll join you," Honey-Lou said. She stood up, smoothed her dress back down over her ass. "Fancy some company?"

Colton smiled but looked unsure. He had meant the room to be for just he and Alicia. And even though she'd not so much as acknowledged his presence this whole time, she was still his wife.

"It's okay, she can come too." Honey-Lou pulled Alicia by the hand from her chair. Alicia stood; her face registered nothing, her eyes remained still and just stared.

"What about them?" Eric asked, looking over at the president and his sickly aide.

"I'll put *him* in there." Chardonnay pointed to a large pet carrier in the corner. "And I really don't think the old boy is going anywhere, do you?" He grasped the president by the thick roll of skin on his neck and pulled him toward the carrier. The president spat and yowled and tried his best to claw at the transvestite's wrists, determined to do harm. The president, however, was unable to voice his protests because his aide had lost consciousness and lay quite still on the floor.

Chardonnay slammed the crate door closed and settled himself back down in the single armchair in the small room.

"Before you turn in," he said to Colton. "Perhaps you might like a little fun?"

Colton looked at the man and was forced to admit he did look hot in his sexy businesswoman getup. He'd shaved his legs glassy smooth, his arms too, and Colton was certain the long, glossy hair was no wig.

"I've been cooped up in this place for days with no one to play with." His eyes burned into Colton's. He stroked a meaty hand over his leg, pulling the pencil skirt up to show a little more of his silky thigh.

Colton felt a stirring in his groin. Despite everything he had just been through, he was actually getting turned on by this man-mountain in women's clothing. *To his credit*, Colton thought, *he did look kind of attractive in the cottage's half-light and whilst the breasts were obviously implants, tits were tits at the end of the day.*

"We could have a lot of fun together," Chardonnay purred. "You, me, your girlfriends." A smile. "Hell, I'd even give your dog a good time." He uncrossed his legs and leaned back in the chair, thighs parted, genitals dangling. "As you can see, I'm a big girl."

And there it was, moment ruined. Colton felt his semi-erection deflate at an alarming speed. His mind imagined one of those cartoons where they stick a hole in the cat, and it farts all over the room like a balloon as the air comes out of it. Somehow, the juxtaposition of being a big girl with a fat black dick didn't sit well with his drive right now. Colton attempted a smile, searching for an excuse to just leave the room.

"Don't worry, Colton," Eric chirped. "I got this." He padded across the room, his lipstick cock already out, red and shiny. He buried his head under Chardonnay's skirt and suckled at the transvestite's meaty dick.

"Thanks, Eric," Colton said.

"Thank *you*," Chardonnay moaned, already in the throes of euphoria.

Honey-Lou led Alicia and Colton to the remaining bedroom. There, she pulled Alicia onto the large, comfortable bed and undressed her; the flimsy robe slipped from her shoulders. Honey-Lou wrinkled her nose at the blood-stained sleeve. Although the blood was dry, it still made her cringe to know it came from the old man who was dying in the next room. She lay Alicia down, her eyes feasting on the woman's perfect pale skin and her pert breasts topped with jutting rose-pink nipples. Honey-Lou stole a glance downward at the smooth lips of Alicia's vulva that puffed up from between her slightly parted thighs.

"I can see why you loved her so much," Honey-Lou said to Colton as she slipped off her own pink dress and lay down naked on the bed next to Alicia. "She really is beautiful." She licked a finger and traced it around one of Alicia's nipples and smiled as it stiffened to her touch. "See, she does know what's going on."

Colton undressed, a sinking feeling in his stomach in direct contrast to the fierce erection he had going on. Something about this scenario felt so absolutely *wrong*, yet the thought of sinking his dick into his Alicia's pussy again felt so absolutely right. Colton climbed onto the bed next to his wife and watched as Honey-Lou seduced her.

Honey-Lou massaged Alicia's breasts a while, planted tender kisses over her body as she did so, and waited with patience for the reciprocal response that wasn't forthcoming. She kissed her way down from between Alicia's breasts, paused to probe her navel with an exploring tongue and then onward down to Alicia's hairless pussy. Colton stroked his wife's hair as Honey-Lou's bald head made its way down the length of her body. He was hoping for some response, some sign in his wife's eyes that she knew he was there; that the Alicia he knew and loved and lusted after was still alive in this beautiful but soulless shell.

Honey-Lou grasped Colton's dick with a suddenness that made him gasp. With slow, deliberate strokes, she began to masturbate him, keen that he feel included in the *ménage*. Honey-Lou parted Alicia's legs with a gentle pressure, eager to gain access to the sweet, fragrant sex nestled between. Once exposed, she lapped at Alicia's clitoris, circled it with her tongue, and sucked it gently into her mouth. It tasted so good, sweet like some exotic fruit, and felt slippery in her mouth. She flicked her tongue along the ridges of Alicia's labia tasting the salty tang of the warm flesh and inhaled deeply through her nose to take in the feminine bouquet. Honey-Lou could feel her own juices flowing as her Bartholin's gland went into overdrive, and the dampness that spread between her own clenched thighs.

She imagined that she felt Alicia's pelvis rise upward. Only slightly, but perhaps it was some response to the probing tongue that dipped into her bubbling, wet vagina. Encouraged by this, Honey-Lou tongue-fucked Alicia, delighting in the feel of the soft ridges at the entrance of the sweet-tasting hole.

Colton kissed his wife, eager for the same reaction he'd gotten in the SUV. And, sure enough, Alicia's lips pressed against his, her tongue probed his mouth, and her teeth nibbled at his lips like he remembered she used to.

Just how he liked it.

A noise; a bubbling, gurgling sound and a shriek of disgust from Honey-Lou followed by an unmistakable reek invaded Colton's nostrils.

Alicia's bowels had let go full blast in Honey-Lou's face. Honey-Lou sat up on the bed, her face smeared with liquid shit. She had a look of shock in her eyes but licked her lips with a lascivious grin. Sweet Jesus, was there nothing that woman didn't find sexual? At this point, Colton began feeling like he was about to vomit, but to his shame, he ejaculated in Honey-Lou's hand at the sight of her shit-smeared face.

As if to add to Colton's misery, the sounds of Eric and Chardonnay's coupling in the next room filtered through the thin walls, and Colton couldn't help but conjure the mental imagery of his dog/son humping away at the big transvestite, his bulbous doggy dick sliding in and out of the wannabe woman's bulbous, wobbling booty.

His sweet, sexy Alicia just lay there on the bed before him. Her eyes stared unblinking from a face without expression, and the rise and fall of her breasts was almost the only indicator that his wife was still alive.

***

A light shone in Colton's left eye.

It was bright and painfully burning to an eye that had spent so long in complete darkness.

"I think we have a response," a disembodied voice said, then the harsh light moved on to shine into Colton's right eye.

Colton forced himself back to consciousness, more than relieved to be away from the growing nightmare of his dream despite the fiery pain that wracked his body. Sadly, the bittersweet memory of his catatonic dream wife had come with him into his waking state and that marched his psyche toward the deep pit of depression.

"There is most definitely some pupil dilation," the voice boomed, and Colton strained to see its owner. Unfortunately, he could only make out that he was staring up someone's nostrils. "Both pupils too. Not much, I know, but I think at this stage, it's a good sign." The light went away, along with the nostrils and their thick, wiry hairs with the flakes of dried snot that clung to them.

As he struggled to consciousness, Colton became aware of the monotonous *beep-beep-beep* of the life-support machines keeping him alive. He found their electronic beeps were strangely comforting, and they sure beat the hell out of listening to the sounds he'd left behind in the cottage; Eric's yelps of delight, Chardonnay's gruff, animal grunts, and Alicia's bowel movement. *Yes indeed, it was wonderful to be back in the real world*, Colton thought.

He tried to move, but the heavy bandages and casts on his body, along with the muscle relaxants they pumped into him via one of the many IV drips that stood sentry around his bed, prevented that. All Colton's efforts succeeded in doing was to create more bolts of pain that shot through his body like molten bullets. He couldn't speak, of course, because he still had the breathing tube rammed down his throat, so all he could do was stare at the mottled Styrofoam ceiling tiles and hope the doctors, nurses, or whoever was responsible for shining lights in his eyes, would spot that he was actually awake.

"Give him twenty CCs of pentobarbital," the voice said. "We need to keep him under for the time being."

Colton began to panic. They couldn't possibly be thinking of a medically induced coma? He'd just woken up!

Noooo! his mind screamed out, but of course, they couldn't possibly hear him.

"Thank you," the owner of the voice said. Colton felt a miniscule tug on the cannula that stuck out from his arm and the chill of cool liquid in his veins. Gradually, the ceiling tiles began to fade into the murky gray.

***

There was panic in the cottage. Raised voices, running feet, and guns loading.

"We gotta go!" Colton heard Zack shouting. "Now!"

Colton dragged his ass off the bed. The soiled bedspread was gone because Honey-Lou had thrown it outside after Alicia's accident. Alicia and Honey-Lou were still there, however, one on either side of him. He had no idea of how long they had all been laying there in that tiny bedroom, nor did Colton have a clue as to what had occurred after Alicia had inadvertently shat in Honey-Lou's face; although, he could guess enough time had elapsed to have gotten the two women cleaned up.

And now there was this.

They threw on their clothes. Honey-Lou helped Alicia back into her bloodied gown and joined Zack and the others in the living room.

"They've found us," Zack told them. "Time we weren't here." He had President Ocelot in the pet carrier by his side. The president stared out at the Resistance leader like he was gloating at their imminent capture. "I'm gonna need some help carrying this out." He looked at Colton.

"Yeah, sure," Colton agreed.

"What about him?" Honey-Lou looked toward the recumbent aide. "We can't just leave him here."

"He's dead and gone, sugar," Chardonnay informed the bald girl. "Must have slipped away while Eric and I were having some fun." He cupped his own balls and winked at Eric who flushed a little and smiled.

Colton shuddered to think the last thing the president's elderly aide had heard in the final moments of his life were the orgasmic grunts and groans of an oversized cross-dresser and a dog/human hybrid. *Rather him than me,* Colton thought.

It was still dark outside, although the first cracks of dawn were threatening the night sky. Zack and Colton ventured out from the relative sanctuary of the cottage and maneuvered the pet carrier into the rear of the SUV. Honey-Lou kindly helped a stumbling Alicia into the vehicle, and Eric bounded in after them.

Zack climbed into the driver's seat, gunned the engine, and the SUV sprang to life; its engine all but drowned out by the *thud-thud-thud* of an approaching helicopter.

"We're waiting for you, Chardonnay," he shouted to the transvestite.

Chardonnay appeared at the cottage doorway and looked immaculate in a black Chanel pant suit, accessorized by exquisite, patent-black Jimmy Choo pumps and the subtlest of gold chain jewelry. In his hand, he carried a cell phone.

"Somebody's gotta chair the welcoming committee, hun," Chardonnay hollered back.

"You were supposed to set them all on timers," Zack shouted with a sad resignation in his voice. "You asshole."

"Not enough time," the transvestite smiled back. He glanced up at the chopper that hovered overhead, its downdraft whipping the treetops into a frenzy. He waved up at the black-uniformed guard leaning out, sniper rifle to his eye.

Zack weighed his options, realized he didn't have any and waved farewell to one of his best operatives.

"You stubborn, dumb fuck," Zack shouted.

Chardonnay didn't—couldn't—hear Zack. With the thrumming sound of the helicopter and the cacophony of the approaching armored vehicles that crashed through the forest toward the cottage, he could barely hear anything at all.

Zack sped the SUV away from the cottage back along the bumpy dirt road. In his rearview mirror, he could see the dark-gray armored vehicles surround the cottage and close in on Chardonnay, who stood defiant on the front porch. One of the armored vehicles broke rank and set off after Zack's SUV. To his surprise, Zack saw it gain ground with an alarming speed despite its bulk.

Colton grimaced as he was bounced around the SUV. He still ached from the inward journey and hadn't had time to rest up what with the disastrous attempt at a three-way with his brain-dead wife and the insatiable Honey-Lou Woolston, and, not to mention, his all-too brief, frustrating flirtation with the real world. *At least*, Colton consoled himself, *he didn't have the dying groans of the president's aide to put up with on this leg of the journey.*

Eric wound down his window and stuck out his head—as dogs are wont to do—to watch the armored vehicle chase their SUV.

"Put your head back in the car!" Zack screamed at him.

"Why?" Eric queried.

As if on cue, the cottage exploded. The flash of light was blinding in the darkness of the early morning and reminded Colton of the harsh light the doctors had shone in his eyes. The light from the explosion seemed to flare in all directions at once, and the fireball engulfed the forest surrounding the cottage, presidential armored vehicles and all. As the intense heat hit the armored cars, each one blew up in sequence like fireworks on the Fourth of July. The blazing explosion even reached the helicopter, and it spiraled down to the forest floor in flames where it created its own fireball amongst the trees.

The sound of the explosion and the accompanying shockwave hit the SUV moments later; a split second or two after Eric had put his head back into the vehicle and hit the button to wind up his window. The SUV rocked and swerved as Zack fought against the hot, buffeting air to keep it on the dirt path. The armored vehicle behind them fared less well, however. The shockwave hit it hard and, whilst it remained on the road, its occupants were reduced to mush. As Eric, Colton, and the others watched, the armored vehicle trickled to a slow stop and just sat there, dead on the road.

"Thank you, Chardonnay," Zack said beneath his breath. "I owe ya."

The SUV left the dirt road and the thick column of smoke rising up from the forest behind it, and made its way to the main road. Zack kept his foot pressed hard to the metal, determined to get back to headquarters before daylight broke.

CHAPTER TEN

They hit the first roadblock around twelve miles along the road. There was a makeshift barrier across both carriageways and a massive amount of presidential guards patrolling it. Zack eased the SUV to a crawl and pulled into the line behind a red Corvette.

"Okay, Mr. President," he said, "here's how we're going play this." He turned to face the pet carrier. President Ocelot, mute without his aide, glowered at Zack with hate-filled eyes. "You are going use your superpowers, or whatever it is that you do with your mind tricks, to get us through this," Zack continued. "And in return, Honey-Lou won't blow your fucking head off."

Zack stared at the President, unsure of what to make of the look on the cat's face. There were two choices here, and whichever one went down pretty much depended on President Ocelot's sense of self-preservation.

Colton looked over at Honey-Lou who seemed to be enjoying her new role as urban terrorist. She poked the muzzle of her gun through the bars at the front of the president's crate and grinned at her prisoner.

"Just say the word, and I'll blow the motherfucker to hell and back," Honey-Lou growled, and Colton felt his dick twitch.

"Do nothing until I say so," Zack said. "Killing him will be our last resort. If we're all going to die here anyway, at least we get to take him with us." Zack eyeballed Colton and Eric. "If it comes down to it, and they take out Honey-Lou and me, it's up to you guys to do what's right."

Colton nodded, although he was actually a little unsure as to exactly what the right thing to do would be in these circumstances. He looked over at Eric, who simply nodded like a crazy person; of course, he'd be more than happy to put paid to a cat.

A guard approached the SUV and shone his flashlight into Zack's face. Zack kept his face deadpan straight and barely acknowledged the guard. The guard paced around the vehicle and probed the interior with his flashlight beam. The light illuminated Alicia, Eric, and then moved on to Colton.

Colton froze. Should he smile, wave, do nothing? Having never been in a situation like this before—in dreams *or* real life—Colton genuinely had no idea. He settled on a passive stare, and, for some reason unknown to himself, he felt it the natural thing to do to put a protective arm around Alicia.

The guard's flashlight lit up Honey-Lou's face next. She stared defiantly into the light, her eyes bright and menacing. The guard played the light over her over naked head and bulging tits a while and then moved on to the pet carrier and the cold reflective eyes of the president.

In that split second, Colton experienced the greatest surge of terror he'd ever known. The entire surface of his skin broke out with a prickly sweat, and his heart pounded so loud in his chest that he was convinced the guard would actually be able to hear it. He closed his eyes, not wanting to witness the point at which the inevitable bullets began fly.

If you die in a dream...

The guard thumped twice on the roof of the SUV to move it on, and Colton almost shit in his pants. Zack pulled away as the barrier lifted for him, and within a heartbeat or two, they were free and clear and on their way.

"Jesus, shit that was close." Eric broke the silence.

"Fuck, yeah." Honey-Lou exhaled. She rested the gun across her knees and wiped her damp palms on her dress. "He looked straight at the president. I thought we were all fucked right then and there."

"I guess the old mind control does work," Zack allowed himself a relieved laugh.

Mind control, Colton mused. It put him in mind of a movie he'd seen in a different lifetime; the one with the fake moon that blew shit up, some tall yeti thing that sounded like a car failing to start, and the brother and sister who made out by accident.

This is not the presidential ocelot you are looking for.

Colton decided to keep his arm around Alicia since he enjoyed having her close no matter how stiff and cold she presented. *Although, there's something slightly different about her now*, he told himself; was she a little less rigid, was that the slightest hint of a smile on her lips, or was it simply the light of the breaking dawn on her heavenly face? Either way, Colton would take it; just being close to his wonderful wife was enough for now.

***

Zack got them to the Resistance headquarters a few hours later. After the ball-shrinking terror at the roadblock, he'd made the decision to take the quieter back roads; there was no reason to court detection in the name of saving a little time. That strategy had added an hour or so to the journey on bumpy, ill-maintained roads, but no one had complained.

Colton climbed out of the SUV with a groan. His joints were stiff, his back ached, and he didn't think he would *ever* get the stink of the combined fear sweat of five people out of his sinuses.

"A little help, Colton?" Zack called him over. Between them, Colton and Zack moved the president's carrier into the building.

There was rapturous applause upon their arrival. Every member of the Resistance had turned out to see the triumphant return of Zack Stackhouse, his team, and, of course, one incredibly humbled president. They all filled the main atrium of the building and flowed out into the hallways that fed into it, crammed shoulder to shoulder, all smiles and pride.

Zack raised his hands for a silence that came after a while. "Thank you!" his raised voice sounded a little croaky. "Without the hard work and support of everyone here, it would not have been possible to achieve our objective." He tapped the carrier with his foot. "The Resistance is not a collection of individuals; it is one body and one mind." Again, the applause, cheers, and whistles were deafening.

Colton thought Zack seemed uncomfortable with the adulation of his people; he almost looked as if he felt he didn't deserve the outpouring of love. Maybe he felt that such gaiety was ill timed considering not all of the team had returned; people had lost their lives for the sake of the Big Plan—*his* Big Plan. Or perhaps, it was simply because the man was exhausted.

Zack's triumphant address to his followers was brief and to the point. After thanking them all for their unwavering support, he asked that they take a little time to remember those who had lost their lives. He finished on a high with the promise that they could begin to make the changes they had all been fighting for now that they had the president in their hands. And he promised them a celebration party to beat all celebration parties. Zack—ever the skilled orator—had left them inspired yet wanting more.

The gathered crowd had still been cheering when Zack, Colton, and the others took the president to one of the interrogation cells that doubled as a play-torture room on orgy nights. There was a rack in one corner and shackles and chains hung from the plain walls. Once inside, Zack opened the door to the pet carrier to let the president out.

"Make yourself at home, Mr. President," Zack said. "I'll catch up with you in a little while and then we can have a good old chin-wag." He allowed himself a wry chuckle and then he and Colton stepped out of the cell and locked the door behind them. Colton peered through the small window set into the door and saw the president cowering in the crate, reluctant to leave one prison for another.

Colton took Alicia back to his quarters to rest up. First thing's first, he helped her to shower. He relieved his wife of the grubby, bloodstained gown and guided her into the hot shower. Colton got naked and joined her under the stinging heat. He lovingly soaped and scrubbed Alicia's body like in the days gone by when they were lovers, caressing her skin with his soapy hands and trying not to prod her too hard in the thigh with his erection. Colton then cleaned himself up and shaved his rough face with a disposable razor. All the while, Alicia stood expressionless and impassive in the steaming stream of water.

After the shower, Colton dried Alicia off and sat her down on the edge of the bed as he dressed, and he wondered what he should dress his wife in. Perfectly on cue, there was a polite knock on his door.

"It's me, Colton; Honey-Lou," a muffled voice said. "Are you guys decent?"

Colton cracked a wry smile at this. After everything he and Honey-Lou had been through together, decency was the last thing either of them ought to be worried about right now.

"Sure," he said, and Honey-Lou came in.

"I brought some clothes for Alicia." Honey-Lou off-loaded a pile of clothes onto the bed. "I hope they fit."

Colton smiled and told her he was sure they would fit just fine. She and Alicia were of similar height and build, and whilst Alicia had not been adverse to moments of exhibitionism in the past, he was pleased to see that Honey-Lou had brought along a slightly more demure selection with which to dress his wife. The Resistance, who had thought of practically everything for Colton and his accidental companions, had not anticipated Alicia's presence and so had not provided him with any women's clothes.

Honey-Lou kissed Colton softly on the mouth and then likewise Alicia. Colton contemplated Honey-Lou, and boy, did she look good. She was clean and polished from her own ablutions, and her hairless skin shone with a healthy glow. She was barefoot, as was her preference, and she wore her trademark hotpants; Colton couldn't help but marvel at the way in which the shorts parted her pussy lips and that he could see the faint outline of her inner labia through the flimsy material. Barely covering her tits, she'd stretched a matching white bandeau top around her chest, and her nipples pointed like tiny fingers through the material.

Colton selected an oversized white T-shirt with *FRANKIE SAYS* emblazoned across the chest and began to slip it over Alicia's head.

"Aww, I kinda like her naked," Honey-Lou said and pushed the tee away. She cupped one of Alicia's breasts and twirled the soft nipple around between thumb and forefinger.

"How is she?" Honey-Lou asked.

"Much the same," Colton told her.

Honey-Lou sat down on the bed beside Alicia and stroked her hair.

"That's a pity, Colton," Honey-Lou said. "Although, it must be nice to have your wife back."

"I guess so," Colton replied. "It would be better if she were her old self again. It's like she's not really here at all, like she's just some kind of doll."

"I kinda like the idea of us having a real-life fuck doll to play with." Honey-Lou giggled. She eased a hand between Alicia's legs and began to massage the stiffening clit that greeted her. "I miss Cole," Honey-Lou said, in a quiet voice. "I can't get it out of my head—what happened to him—what they made me do."

"You can't blame yourself, Honey-Lou." Colton knelt at her feet. "You really had no other choice." He parted Honey-Lou's legs and licked his way along her thigh.

"I keep telling myself that, but—" Honey-Lou's voice dissolved into a low moan as Colton's tongue arrived at her cunt, and he probed at it through her pants. She dipped a forefinger into Alicia's pussy and was amazed at just how wet she had gotten so quickly. And as she leaned in to kiss those perfectly soft, plump lips of Alicia's, Honey-Lou was sure she saw a glimmer of recognition, of *something* in the woman's eyes.

***

Zack had finally coaxed President Ocelot out of the crate. Actually, he'd dragged the damned cat out by the scruff of the neck. The president sat on the rack with his tail flicking to and fro at the wrist straps, staring his malevolent stare at Zack.

Zack was accompanied in the interrogation room by one of his most trusted foot soldiers; a squat, shiny-headed, broad-chested guy who went by the name of Anthony. Anthony was fiercely loyal to the cause, a Resistance man through and through, and had a reputation for being a mean sonofabitch. Everyone, even Zack, approached Anthony with the utmost respect and never—ever—shortened his name to Tony. Anthony had made it clear that one always pronounced the '*th*' in his name. Stick to those basics, and Anthony could be the best friend you'd ever have.

"You *are* going to have to speak to us sooner or later," Zack addressed the president. "We have provided you with Anthony here to give you a voice, so there can be no excuses, Mr. President."

"Anything?" he asked Anthony.

The big guy shook his head.

The president glowered at the two of them.

"I don't know how long you intend to keep this up, Mr. President." Zack leaned in close to the cat's face. "But I don't have all day. We are throwing a shindig this evening to celebrate the Resistance getting our hands on you, and I fully intend to be there," he said. "How about you, Anthony?"

"Wouldn't miss it for the world, boss," Anthony replied.

"And, unless we get some answers from you pretty damn quick, you'll never guess who the guest of honor is going to be." Zack threatened. "I always wondered what fricasseed cat meat tasted like." He grinned at the president.

"Chicken'd be my guess. Or maybe pork." Anthony joined in with a deep, rumbling laugh.

And Zack thought he caught a hint of fear in the president's cold, hateful eyes.

***

Colton lay sandwiched between Honey-Lou Woolston and Alicia. Alicia lay on her side with her back to him, and Honey-Lou rubbed her naked body against his back and fingered his asshole with a nimble finger or two. Colton slipped his dick into Alicia's moist, inviting pussy, and a satisfied gasp escaped his lips as her warmth closed around it. Slowly at first, Colton began to slide in and out of his wife, hoping against hope there would be a response from her this time that was not merely mechanical.

Colton tried in vain to clear his head of thoughts of what they had done to his beloved Alicia that made her this way. Had she been clinically dead in the gameshow studio for too long before they revived her to live out her days as the president's plaything? Or had they done something else to her? A lobotomy perhaps—or some brain-frying drug? Whatever it was, Colton couldn't bear the thought of having to see her like this day in and day out, no matter how good her cunt felt, and he began to think about how he could put and end to her suffering.

At this, Colton spasmed and shot a thick load into his wife. Whilst it felt good, the orgasm was nothing like he remembered his climaxes with Alicia to be. It was simply not the same without her powerful pussy gripping him and squeezing out every drop of his cum.

"My turn." Honey-Lou rolled Colton over; his cock slipped out of Alicia and she let out a barely audible moan. Honey-Lou climbed on top of Colton and positioned herself over his glistening dick.

"Did you hear that?" Colton asked her.

"Did I hear what?" Honey-Lou replied as she lowered her puckered ass onto the swollen head.

"I think Alicia just made a noise," Colton sounded excited.

"Most likely just air coming out of her pussy." Honey-Lou smiled. "It happens." She sank herself down onto Colton's penis and concentrated hard on relaxing the muscles necessary to allow him to penetrate deep into her ass. She gasped and rolled her eyes with pleasure as she rested her weight on him and enjoyed the feel of him inside of her body.

"I know what a queef sounds like, Honey-Lou." Colton defended. "And I am sure Alicia just moaned. She hasn't made any kind of noise like that since—"

Honey-Lou cut him off with a well-timed hand to his throat. She squeezed tight to cut off his breath and Colton's face turned red. Just how he liked it. Ignoring the silent Alicia, who just lay there next to Colton, Honey-Lou rocked her pelvis with jerking motions that drove Colton's dick deep into her bowel and ground her clit against his pubic bone.

Colton embraced the sudden lack of air, the rapidly depleting oxygen in his body would—he knew from experience with erotic asphyxiation—guarantee a mind-blowing climax he hoped would compensate for the rather unimpressive result he'd had with his wife. Colton pressed his hips upward to penetrate Honey-Lou's rectum further, even though he was already buried so deep inside he could feel the roughness of her next bowel movement as it scraped against his dick.

Alicia moaned again. Colton paused, much to Honey-Lou's annoyance. He put a finger to Honey-Lou's lips to shush her. Alicia made a slight movement next to him, and her butt pressed into his hip. It was as if she was offering herself to him. As if she wanted her husband's cock back inside her.

"I think you are imagining things, mister," Honey-Lou said, doing her best to hide the impatience in her voice. She wriggled her ass which elicited a strangled groan from Colton, and then she continued fucking him.

Neither of them noticed, as they ass-fucked each other to euphoria, that Alicia's hand had wandered down to stroke her own denuded pussy.

***

"I'll ask you again, Mr. President." Zack ran a hand through his thicket of unruly hair. "Why do you persecute the Dreamers?"

President Ocelot just stared him down.

"We know you can do it, so why don't you just use Anthony here to answer my fucking questions, and we can be through?" Zack's temper was beginning to show. He felt as though he was losing this particular battle of wills, and he hated to lose at anything. And, whilst he was prepared to go the distance and break the president down over as long as it took, he desperately wanted at least a few answers for his people before the day was out. And besides, he didn't want to disappoint everyone at the big celebration. To have gone through all of the planning and preparation of the Big Plan, and the subsequent execution thereof, to have lost good men only to be met with this stony silence, would be anticlimactic to say the least.

"Okay, Mr. President." Zack pulled out a pair of pliers from his pocket. "I didn't want to have to go down this road, but you really are not throwing me any crumbs here." He advanced on the president, who now cowered against the hard leather top of the rack. "Hold the fucker down, Anthony."

***

Colton came with a guttural grunt and ejaculated inside Honey-Lou's ass with such a force that it felt like his guts were squirting out of his dick. For a second or two, a fleeting thought of the Devil's Roulette Ball shot across his mind, and he had to remind himself he was on the right side of the twelve hours—just. Honey-Lou was hot on his heels with her own orgasm, and she screamed blue murder as she came. She rolled her eyes and scratched at Colton's chest, and her own tits like a thing possessed.

"Fuck!" she yowled as she ground her pussy hard against Colton to squeeze out the last drops of orgasm from her tender clitoris. She could feel Colton twitch and jump inside of her as his cock spat the last dregs of come into her rectum, and boy-fucking-howdy, did that feel good! Honey-Lou collapsed on top of Colton, and he held her. The sweat from their exertions mingled and mixed with the scent of their sex and the faint, sweet smell of her shit. Colton sighed as he felt himself slowly deflate inside Honey-Lou's body.

On the bed beside them, Alicia stirred, and let out a soft mewl.

Honey-Lou slid off of Colton; this time she *had* heard something. She rested her head on her hand on Colton's chest and watched Alicia.

"You heard that too?" Colton asked.

"Yep."

"Alicia? Honey?" Colton reached over and shook his wife's shoulder. "It's me, Colton—and Honey-Lou," he coaxed. "You remember Honey—"

Alicia sat up with a start, her eyes wide and darting. Blood poured from her mouth, and she lifted her hands to her face. Then, she let out an unearthly scream.

"That fucking hurt!" Alicia wailed. "You *fuckers*!"

"I'm sorry, babe," Colton tried to console his wife. "We didn't mean to upset you." He caressed her face with his fingertips and smeared the blood across her cheek.

"Hello, baby." Alicia faced Colton and for the first time, he saw the glimmer of *his* Alicia in her eyes. "Did you see me on the TV?" She took her hands down from her face and smiled him a sweet, bloody smile. "I did it for you," she purred. "Now would you please get me to Zack before he pulls out any more of my fucking teeth?"

CHAPTER ELEVEN

The incessant beeping of the machines by the bed stirred Colton from his drug-induced slumber. He tried to open his eyes but found he couldn't. Either they had taped them closed again, or the relaxant drugs were still in effect. Most likely the latter, he guessed, since his eyelids weren't the only part of him that was immobile; thus far, pretty much everything had refused to do as he asked; the paralysis still dominated his body.

There was the plus that the pain wasn't so bad this time around, which may have been due to the drugs, or the miracle of his body's own healing process. *No way of telling at this stage*, he told himself, *best just go with what you've got.*

"His vitals are looking good, Mrs. Forshay," a now familiar voice cut through the darkness.

"So I see," Zeenah's voice rang out. Colton caught a whiff of her perfume as she walked by, and it made him want to retch. He'd never liked that particular perfume. Partly because she'd told him it was a gift from a friend but had never divulged which friend, and partly because it had undertones of cat piss.

"Oh, I'm sorry about that, Mrs. Forshay," the voice apologized. "John, get a nurse in to clean this up, will you?"

"On it," a third voice replied from what could have been another room.

"Must have been one doozy of a wet dream my husband was having, Doctor?" Zeenah said.

Was that flirtatiousness in her voice? Really?

"It's not uncommon, Mrs. Forshay, it happens a lot in cases like your husband's," the voice said. "It's usually a sign that things are improving."

"Oh," Colton heard Zeenah reply.

Oh?

Was that it? *Oh?* Could the vile woman not even try to hide the disappointment in her voice? Colton strained his brain to conjure up an image of Zeenah, but he could only see Alicia's face smiling back at him. And he couldn't remember the last time Zeenah had smiled at him like that.

"We'll be decreasing the pentobarbital over the next few days; he should be able to breathe by himself by then."

"And then?" Zeenah's voice again.

"And then your husband will be conscious and hopefully on the way to recovery."

"That's wonderful, Doctor, thank you." Could she have said the word *wonderful* with any less disgust in it?

"Are you coming, honey?" Colton heard Zachary Stackhouse's voice. "We only put an hour in the meter."

"Coming, babe," Zeenah replied in that sing-song voice of hers that was once reserved only for Colton.

Colton sighed to himself. It had been a long, long time since Zeenah had called *him* babe.

***

Zack was beside himself when Colton and Honey-Lou took Alicia down to see him. He welcomed them into the interrogation room and introduced them to Anthony with all the eagerness of a new kid at school.

"And you've met President Ocelot, of course," Zack finished up.

"Mr. President." Colton nodded at the wild cat. He noted it had blood matted in the fur on its chin which was eerily reminiscent of the blood that had poured from his wife's mouth earlier.

Alicia had dressed herself, much to Colton's amazement; she'd gone from catatonic to alive and kicking in a matter of moments. She wore the *RELAX* T-shirt that came down to her mid-thigh and nothing else. She had decided against panties, as the ones Honey-Lou had brought for her were a size too large, much to Honey-Lou's chagrin.

"Now that you have found a voice, Mr. President, we may be getting somewhere," Zack said. He motioned for Anthony to stand up and guided Alicia to the chair. She sat down.

"That we might," the president said through Alicia's mouth. "You certainly have gone to a lot of trouble, Mr. Stackhouse."

"So have you, Mr. President," Zack said. "You have set up an entire infrastructure to hunt down and murder those who have The Dream, and I am interested to know why."

"I can imagine that you are," President Ocelot laughed, only it was Alicia's laugh, and hearing it made Colton sad as he realized it wasn't his wife's laugh at all.

"So?" Zack pushed.

"Not with an audience, Mr. Stackhouse," the president told him. "There are things I need to tell you that—others—shouldn't hear." He spat *others* with a great deal of derision.

"If you wouldn't mind?" Zack said, nodded toward Colton, Honey-Lou, and Anthony, then to the door.

Anthony ushered Colton and Honey-Lou out of the interrogation room and then took up his post in the hallway as guardian of the door. Colton left with great reluctance; he didn't want to leave Alicia alone with the president or Zack, the latter having too many links with his real world. But Anthony was insistent by sheer size alone, and Colton had figured it wise to follow Honey-Lou out of the room.

"Don't worry, Colton," Zack winked at him as he left. "I'll take good care of Alicia." They were words that, coming from anyone other than Zack Stackhouse, would have been a comfort. However, it was the last thing Colton wanted to hear right now.

***

They met Eric in the hallway. The interrogation room door had barely closed when he came bounding up in that inimitable, buoyant manner of his; tail all wagging and nails *click-clacking* on the tiled floor.

"Hey, Colton! Hey, Honey-Lou!" Eric greeted them. "I heard about Alicia. That is awesome news!" he said enthused.

Colton cast a glance back at the room behind him.

"Yeah, I guess it is," he replied.

"I came to get Zack for the orgy." Eric grinned. "It's just kicking off now, and you know what they say?" He left it hanging.

"What do they say, Eric?" Honey-Lou took the bait.

"That there's no show without Punch." Eric laughed, and laughed loud.

"I think he's going to be busy a while," Colton said with sadness in his voice.

"C'mon, Colton, quit feeling so sorry for yourself." Honey-Lou gripped his arm. "You should be happy that your Alicia is back, especially now that she seems to be getting better."

"I suppose I should." Colton shrugged. Honey-Lou was right, Alicia *was* back in his life, and yes, he should be grateful for that at least. But this was after two years of him thinking of her as dead. Add to that the knowledge that her newfound animation was only because the president had chosen to use her body as his mouthpiece, and it was cold comfort to him. Colton knew in his heart that his wife would never be the same again, but still he craved to be with her.

"I'm sure they'll be out in no time." Honey-Lou jollied him along. "Zack won't want to miss his own celebration now, will he?"

Again, Colton was forced to agree; Zack's bravery as Resistance leader was easily matched by his ego.

"Just us three, then?" Eric grinned and wagged his tail so hard that it cracked Colton across the balls and made him wince.

"I was going to change clothes for the party," Honey-Lou said.

"Totally unnecessary," Eric told her and sniffed at her crotch with his damp nose. "You look fabulous—as always. And besides, you'll be naked before long—as always." Eric laughed and Honey-Lou shot him a wink.

They followed Eric down the hallway as he bounded along with a definite spring in his step. Colton hated leaving Alicia behind, but he knew there was nothing he could do but hope Zack didn't involve her in any of the more brutal aspects of his interrogation techniques. The thought of the blood bubbling from his wife's mouth was still a fresh one, and it worried him.

The celebratory orgy was underway when they arrived at the main atrium. Someone had put up a banner, hurriedly stencilled in green spray paint on a bedsheet:

**CONGRATS TO ZACK!
WE GOT THE PRES'!**

Subtle, Colton thought to himself, *very subtle indeed.*
The atrium was filled with Resistance people, many of whom looked around in eager anticipation when Eric arrived. The look of disappointment on their faces upon seeing that Eric had only brought along Colton and Honey-Lou went undisguised. There were some smiles, though, and a kind soul thrust a bottle of beer into Colton's hand. It was warm, but most welcome, nonetheless. Colton chugged on the tepid drink and waited for the buzz to take him away from thoughts of Alicia.

Although the orgy had not long since started, it was most definitely in full swing. The majority of the participants were in varying states of undress; some already totally stripped getting down and dirty right there on the floor. Some headed toward the playrooms in couples, threesomes, and moresomes, and Colton observed an entire group of nine or ten making their way into the dungeon room from which the mixed screams of agony and ecstasy could be heard.

Colton stepped over a couple of guys who were too engrossed in their sixty-nine to be aware they were causing an obstruction. He looked down at them, envious of their abandon and then across the sea of wanton faces in the room; the orgy was certainly gathering pace in Zack's absence.

"See ya later, guys!" Eric said as he bounded off in search of something to sink his dick into. "Don't do anything I wouldn't do!" He laughed. Colton and Honey-Lou laughed along.

"That makes it a short list," Honey-Lou called after him. "You okay, Colton?" She turned her attention to her pensive lover.

"I will be," Colton replied. "Once I know Alicia is safe."

"I'm sure Zack wouldn't let anything happen to her. You have to trust him." Honey-Lou pressed her breasts into his arm.

"I guess," Colton said. "But what if he decides to torture the president and *that* hurts Alicia?"

"Quit worrying, will you?" There was a note of annoyance in Honey-Lou's voice. "We're here now. May as well enjoy the party."

The woman has a point, albeit made through impatience, thought Colton. Here he was in a crowd of libertine Resistance fighters—all pheromones and libido—with an endless world of sexual opportunities right there in front of his nose, so what right did he have to be so miserable? Colton chastised himself; this was his erotic dream, after all, and he'd be waking up once his real-life doctors allowed him to. Might as well enjoy it while he could before real life crept back in.

Coming, babe.

A young couple approached Colton and his companion through the crowd. They were both dark haired and Native American in descent. They were unbelievably attractive with rounded faces, dark-brown eyes, and amazingly trim bodies. They were naked, of course, and every detail of their firm, muscular bodies was on full display.

"We were wondering if you guys would like to play?" the girl asked with a smile.

"Yes, I think we would. Don't you agree, Colton?" Honey-Lou replied for the both of them.

Colton nodded, and fought against the urge to leave. *Sex was still sex,* he told himself, *no matter how little he was in the mood for it.*

"That is so awesome!" the guy exclaimed. "You guys are our heroes!" He held out a hand. "I'm Dylan. This is my girl, Melody."

He shook Colton's hand and kissed Honey-Lou firmly upon the lips. His gal, Melody, did likewise, and gave Colton's dick a playful squeeze as she did so.

Colton allowed himself to be led toward one of the playrooms with Honey-Lou guiding him through the crowd by the hand as she wove this way and that to keep up with the splendidly naked behinds of Dylan and Melody. Colton had never thought of himself as a hero before, despite his recent escapades. He was just a regular guy dreaming regular dreams who had had little option but to go with the flow. However, if hero status got him playtime with hot young couples such as this, who the fuck was Colton Forshay to complain?

The playroom was already occupied by a group of eight older guys with each one of a different ethnicity. They all stood naked in the center of the room stroking their impressive erections. Either this was planned or their presence simply didn't bother Dylan or Melody, the latter of whom dropped to her hands and knees almost the minute they were all ensconced within the room, and the door had eased shut behind them.

The playroom, in stark contrast to those Colton had seen there on his first night at the Resistance headquarters before, was bare. No equipment, no instruments of torture, nothing save a thick, blue plastic sheet that covered the floor.

"We call this our 'Around the World game.'" Dylan explained. "You two are our Caucasian contingent."

"It's like a United Nations meeting." Melody grinned up at Colton as the eight men encircled her and pointed their cocks towards her face. "Only with more cum." She giggled and took the Chinese guy's dick into her mouth.

Honey-Lou slipped out of her shorts and rolled her skimpy top up over her head. She squeezed herself between the men to join Melody.

"I'm not missing out on this," she laughed. "Come on, Colton, don't be a party pooper, join in!"

Colton stepped out of his pants and jostled his way into the circle between a huge African American guy and a diminutive Inuit who smelled ever so faintly of tuna. Melody grabbed a hold of Colton's dick and tugged on it in a most pleasant fashion as she sucked on the Chinese guys'.

Colton had attended bukkake parties before, back in the day when he and Alicia had been the darlings of the neighborhood party circuit. Many a time he'd watched his gorgeous wife surround herself with as many men as she could find and take their collective semen in her face. And sometimes the men would stand three or four deep just for the privilege. That had never once failed to give Colton a raging hard-on of epic proportions.

Honey-Lou had a dick in each hand and was tugging on each one with enthusiasm. She pulled them closer toward her body, and instead of taking either one in her mouth, she lowered her face and rubbed the cocks on her bald head. This drove the men wild, and when she released them, they took great delight in slapping the smooth skin with their dicks and rolling them across her shiny dome.

Before too long, Colton and the other guys began to utter those tell-tale, pre-orgasm grunts. As each one did so, they maneuvered into position above Melody's face, dicks aimed and good to go. Seeing this, Dylan stepped inside the circle, and took a hold of his girlfriend's head and held open her eyelids.

The Chinese guy groaned and pulled his dick out of Melody's mouth. It came out with a wet popping sound and immediately began to twitch. The Indian guy and Colton jerked themselves hard, and all three began to ejaculate.

Melody let out a squeal of delight as three loads of hot, sticky cum sprayed into her upturned face. Several fat strings of it spat into her eyes which made her squeal even more. Dylan beamed with delight at the sight, and whilst his own dick twitched with an intent of its own, he didn't let go of his girl's face.

Colton marvelled at Melody's ability to take eyefuls of semen without flinching. He'd had a drop or two in his own eyes on past occasions, and he knew just how much that stuff could smart. He let out a deep sigh as the last of his cum splashed onto Melody's chin, and his place was taken by the African American who was dribbling sticky white cum before he could even get into in position.

"Cum for me, people!" Honey-Lou cried out her encouragement at the guys who jerked off on her head; there were three of them now—the original two had since been joined by the Inuit guy. "Cum on my fucking head, you dirty bastards!"

She was really getting into this, Colton thought as he watched her hands rub at her pussy with ferocity, like she was trying to set it on fire.

Colton stepped back out of the circle, his dick still hard, and watched as Honey-Lou took three shots of ejaculate on her head. She moaned loudly with each fresh, hot splash, and keeping one hand rubbing at her clit, Honey-Lou brought the other up to smear the cum over her skull to make it all slimy and shiny wet. Colton couldn't help but stare at the scene; Melody with her staring eyes filled with sticky white cum, and Honey-Lou with her wet, shining head. But, for as arousing as the scenario was, Colton couldn't help but think of Alicia and wish she was here with him to enjoy this.

CHAPTER TWELVE

"So, Zachary, you can see why it is important that my motives for all of this are kept well away from the general populace," President Ocelot said. Alicia Forshay spoke his words in a flat monotone.

Zack was forced to agree, as much as it went against the grain. What the president had just revealed to him not only made great sense, but it did actually seem to carry with it the justification of kidnap, torture, and murder.

"There really is no other way?" Zack pressed, although he knew the answer.

"I'm afraid not," the president said through Alicia. "Lord only knows we tried to find a way around it." A sigh of resignation. "But you can see now why it is in the best interests of everyone involved, including the Dreamers themselves."

Zack leaned against the cool wall and tried to take it all in. The knowledge the president had just imparted weighed heavily on his mind. He knew he would have to speak to

Colton and all of the others, but how would he put it into the right words? It had been a long time since he'd had The Dream himself, so long in fact, that he denied having had it at all. The truth was that he could barely remember what it felt like to feel the frustrating split between two worlds. Still, it lay upon his shoulders as leader of the Resistance to pass on the information in as palatable a form as was humanly possible.

Alicia stood up. The T-shirt clung tight to her body, which was damp with the sweat created from the exertion of being the president's telepathic conduit and rode up her thighs.

"I am pleased we understand one another now, Zachary." Alicia said, more of her own voice coming through now. "I was rather hoping we would."

Zack gave her a blank stare, his thoughts elsewhere. His mind was racing; thoughts of capturing President Ocelot, the years of planning that had gone into it, the daring rescue of countless citizens from the clutches of the president's DEO torture squads.

And all for what?

Alicia removed the T-shirt in one swift movement and stood before Zack as naked as the day she was born. She cupped a breast, lifted it upwards and bent her head to lick at the nipple.

"What the—?" Zack spluttered.

"You don't like?" Alicia asked and returned to lapping at the stiff pink teat.

"Yeah—I mean no—I mean—" Zack struggled.

"I thought this was your favorite thing." Alicia winked at him.

Behind her, President Ocelot viewed Zack with narrowed eyes and flicked his tail back and forth.

Alicia had both breasts in her hands now and was alternating her tongue between nipples. She flicked each one with her tongue to moisten them, pressed them between her lips, and then nipped at them with her teeth to make herself gasp as she delighted in the sharp stab of pain that elicited.

"No," Zack said. "Stop this." There was a distinct lack of conviction in his voice.

Alicia didn't stop this.

"We should fuck now," Alicia/President Ocelot said. "No point in delaying the inevitable, Zachary."

"We can't," Zack told her. He stepped away from the wall, tried to sidestep Alicia's achingly, desirable body, but she blocked him.

"Ah, but we can," the president said. "We should both enjoy this body while we can. It's been a long time since I have had a female vessel to play with."

Alicia let go of her breasts and tugged at Zack's belt. He gave a half-hearted attempt to prevent her from undoing his pants, but once his erection sprang free, it was obvious to both parties this was not going to be a prolonged struggle. She spat a precisely aimed gob of saliva onto Zack's dick and massaged it into the swollen head with expert fingers.

"Stop," Zack's feeble protest went unheeded.

The president settled himself down on the rack and rested his head on his front paws, his eyes transfixed on the scene he was creating with the power of his incredible mind. His gaze met with Zack's; it was important to the ocelot that the Resistance leader knew exactly who was seducing him.

Alicia pressed herself up against Zack and forced him backward against the wall; he could feel her sweat soaking through his shirt. She lifted one leg over his hip to position her cunt over his throbbing dick.

"This is wrong," Zack said with a gasp as he felt the slippery skin of Alicia's pussy caress his dick.

"Shh," Alicia silenced him. "Enjoy."

She lowered herself down on Zack's penis with a sharp intake of breath as it slid deep inside her. Even the awareness that the president was making this happen couldn't dampen Zack's carnal lust. Across the room, the president rolled his eyes as the delightful sensations he shared through Alicia's body filtered back to his brain.

Alicia rocked her pelvis against Zack's, and Zack found he had no choice but to meet her thrusts. There was a heat inside her tight vagina that was almost unbearable, but pleasurably so. He gripped her buttocks and thrust hard into her body, forgetting that, in reality, on some level, he was fucking the President.

"Cum," Alicia purred in Zack's ear.

And cum he did.

"Oh, dear mother of fucking God!" Zack screamed out as wave upon wave of intense orgasm crashed through every one of his nerve endings at once. He dug his fingernails into the soft flesh of Alicia's butt as his legs turned to jelly and threatened to dump him onto the floor. Alicia pressed her weight against Zack to keep him propped against the wall, a contented smile on her lips as she felt Zack's sticky fluid begin to trickle down the inside of her thigh.

Zack groaned as he felt Alicia's kegel muscles squeeze hard on his sensitive cock, and he jerked and twitched again. It felt to him as though Alicia were milking him like her pussy was a dairy machine on a cow's teat. Zack spurted again and again, and when Alicia lowered her leg and pulled away, he saw the spreading trail of blood on her legs. Before he could comprehend what was happening, his dick contracted once more and spurted an arc of bright blood across the interrogation room.

Zack's legs betrayed him, and he slid down the wall and could only watch as his dick continued to ejaculate blood. He felt a nauseating panic rise up to tighten his chest, and he knew it was useless to cry out; even if they could hear him over the din of the orgy in the atrium, all of the interrogation rooms were well soundproofed.

"Welcome to the Devil's Roulette, Zachary," the president laughed through Alicia's mouth. "I hope it is all you expected it to be."

"That's bullshit," Zack said. His voice was weak as his body continued to drain. "It's been well over twelve hours since I was given the drugs at the palace."

"Oh yes, the twelve-hour thing." Alicia giggled. "I'm afraid we so totally lied about that." That giggle again. "The Devil's Roulette drugs don't wear off; they last a lifetime," the president explained. "Which is a pity because the six-fuck rule still applies."

"You're fucking lying," Zack growled as he attempted to crawl toward the door using his hands. He found this impossible as he failed to gain traction in the growing pool of his own blood.

"Does it look like I'm lying?" The president's blunt words sounded almost pleasant coming from the naked Alicia Forshay. "Just look at yourself, Zachary."

Zachary did indeed look at himself. He was forced to admit the president may not be lying after all, as spurt upon spurt of viscous blood jetted from his prick, and with each ejaculation, he grew weaker.

And, as President Ocelot and his puppet Alicia watched, Zachary Stackhouse, leader of the Resistance, bled out through his dick.

***

Honey-Lou led Colton from the playroom with all the *joie de vivre* of a little kid at a petting zoo. Her head was still sticky from the copious amounts of cum she'd solicited, and she had left her scant amount of clothing behind having chosen to remain naked to "save time."

Almost everyone in the atrium was naked now; the floor was filled with sweating, copulating bodies, and the playrooms were crammed to capacity and beyond. The sounds of groans, gasps, and screams of orgasmic euphoria mingled with the slap of skin upon skin, and the wet squish of sex made for the most exquisite background music. Colton stepped around and over the writhing mass of people. He wrinkled his nose at the stink of sweat sex and tried his best not to slip on the puddles of spilled fluids.

He saw a couple—a lady in her sixties and a guy in his twenties—strangling each other as they fucked. She sat astride him with his dick buried deep inside her cunt and both hands so tight around his throat it turned his face an alarming shade of purple. The young guy, in turn, was squeezing the old lady's neck, and her eyes bugged out like they were trying to escape the confines of her skull. Colton gawked at them as he walked on by, mesmerized by the grotesque tableau they presented. As he watched, they orgasmed almost simultaneously as their mouths opened wide in a silent O. It concerned Colton that neither of them seemed willing to let go of the other's throat, even as their orgasms subsided, and he wondered if perhaps he should intervene. Before he could decide, Honey-Lou pulled on Colton's arm eager to get to the next playroom. With some reluctance, and a little relief, Colton allowed himself to be dragged away.

"This one looks fun," Honey-Lou snickered as they came upon a half-open playroom door. Inside was a kiddie's paddling pool filled to twelve inches with what appeared to be fresh urine. As they neared the door, Colton caught the distinctive, acrid ammonia whiff that confirmed his suspicion. He peeked into the packed room and saw two women sitting on top of a man in the paddling pool. His body and head were totally submerged face down in the piss and his arms and legs flailed and splashed—much to the delight of the audience.

"Not for me, sorry," Colton said amidst the cheers. "Can we try another room?"

"I guess," Honey-Lou said with more than a little disappointment in her voice.

They left the doorway along with its stink and raucous cheers, and from the corner of his eye, Colton saw them lift the guy's lifeless corpse from the paddling pool and throw it on a pile in the corner, which already comprised a dozen or so others. By the time the next volunteer had stepped up, a fresh-faced young lady not much past her teens, Colton and Honey-Lou were at the next playroom.

"This one." Honey-Lou grinned at Colton and pulled him into the playroom. It was larger than the previous room and busy with naked people. Some of them were there as voyeurs and some were doing their own thing alone or with companions; others were willing participants in the sickening debauchery within.

On one side of the room, a woman with, tragically, ginger hair was strapped into an old-style gynecological chair. Her legs were parted and lifted high by the attached steel stirrups. She had her vagina stretched wide open by a stainless-steel speculum that twinkled in the light reflected from the overhead fluorescents. Colton peered through the group of nude bodies crowded around the chair and saw a rake thin, gray-haired guy scooping what appeared to be red sand from a zinc bucket and carefully pouring it into the lady's gaping pussy.

Ants.

He'd been mistaken; it was not sand at all but hundreds, thousands of shiny red fire ants that jostled and squirmed with liquid movement inside the ginger woman's vulnerable, pink flesh. The woman screamed as the ants crawled inside her and began to bite. Her pained ululation resounded through the room, much to the delight of her audience. They shuffled closer in order to better observe her agony; each one the guys masturbated with an astounding ferocity, and the gals finger fucked themselves with rough thrusts that brought blood from their vaginas. It seemed to Colton they were all desperate to cum before the ant-woman went into shock, and her arousing cries were silenced.

Honey-Lou paid little attention to the ginger lady since formicophillia was clearly not her thing. Her focus was very much on the low table on the opposite side of the room. She wriggled her body between a guy and a girl who stood face to face French kissing with vigor and squirmed their bodies against each other. As Honey-Lou parted them with her lithe, nude body and paused to slip her tongue into the girl's mouth, Colton saw the girl had her partner's dick between her legs and was jerking him with her pussy lips. As the guy pulled away, Honey-Lou reached behind herself and gave the moistened cock a squeeze. She broke off her kiss with the girl and continued on toward the table, tugging on Colton's hand for him to hurry along. Colton slid between the couple with an apologetic smile, and he felt the girl's breasts press against his chest and her man's hard dick prod against his butt.

There was a girl and a man copulating on the low table. She had spiky, short, brunette hair and mountainous—but so obviously fake—tits and milky white skin. Her man was short, a little overweight, and, like Honey-Lou, devoid of any hair whatsoever.

Colton watched as the guy pumped his pelvis up and down on the brunette. Each thrust brought forth an impassioned grunt from each of the pair along with the occasional pained cry. As he and Honey-Lou pushed their way to the front of the observing crowd, Colton could see that there was blood flowing free and fresh from between the woman's thighs and each thrust of the guy's dick seemed to pump more blood out of her. The blood ran in a viscid torrent down along and over the edge of the table where it collected in a plastic bowl. Against the wall next to the table, there were a half dozen similar bowls filled with blood.

"Awesome! It's a light bulb challenge!" Honey-Lou announced with glee. She pointed at the gray wire that trailed out from the woman's pussy and into a wall outlet. "This is so fucking hot." She unzipped Colton's fly and fished out his dick. Keeping her eyes on the bloodied couple, Honey-Lou pressed her back tight into Colton, and eased his penis between her butt cheeks. And while their respective heights prevented penetration of Honey-Lou's most desirable butt hole, Colton enjoyed the enveloping sensation of his dick sandwiched in her warm, muscular crack. Slowly at first, Honey-Lou began to grind herself against Colton.

The brunette lady stopped crying out after another minute or so and ceased moving altogether shortly after that. Undeterred, the guy carried on with his fucking determined to reach his own release no matter what. Colton could feel himself nearing the point of no return with Honey-Lou's butt dry hump, and he absently wondered whether he or the guy with the blood-soaked crotch would cum first.

There was an anticlimactic grunt and a final thrust or two, and the guy was done. He climbed off the woman on the table and almost knocked over the blood bowl by his feet. The guy's penis was a shredded mess; it hung limp between his legs and pumped blood from its tattered skin and torn meat. Were it not for the thin shards of glass that protruded from it, one would think that some rabid animal had chewed on it.

The guy glanced at the unconscious woman, then at his ravaged dick, and then collapsed to his knees. He threw up against the wall, and his body heaved with each wave of nausea. As it transpired, the guy beat Colton to ejaculation only by a matter of a few seconds. Colton gripped Honey-Lou's shoulders as he came in silence, and his jizz spurted between her buttocks, onto her pussy lips, and dribbled onto the floor.

A couple of guys helped the man with the shredded dick away. They had to support him as his legs had given up, and his feet smeared the blood that poured from his ruined cock across the floor. An older couple lifted the brunette from the table and carried her away, having first unplugged the cord from the wall outlet. Colton was not a hundred percent certain, but the woman looked to be dead, or pretty damn close to death's door. Her vagina continued to leak blood as she was carted off to the body pile in the corner.

"Me next!" Honey-Lou leapt forward. She elbowed her way through the next pair of volunteers and jumped onto the table. The two girls next in line glowered at Honey-Lou and muttered their annoyance at the brash, bald girl who had stolen their place. Colton smiled at his friend, and she smiled back at him with that curl of her sweet lips that never failed to make his dick twitch. Although Colton knew what was coming next, it never actually occurred to him to stop her; here, it didn't seem abnormal.

Honey-Lou lay herself down on the table, knees up, and legs parted. A tall, broad-shouldered man dressed head to toe in a black leather gimp suit complete with gas mask approached the table. In his gloved hand, he carried a bare light bulb with a trailing flex. Honey-Lou nodded at the man, and he pressed the bulb against her pussy hole. Colton could see that Honey-Lou was slick from his own cum and that aided the progress of the bulb up into her vagina.

Gimp Suit pushed the light bulb deep up into Honey-Lou, and she wiggled with delight. He then plugged the wire into the outlet by the edge of the table. Another nod from Honey-Lou, and he flicked the switch. Colton and the gathered bystanders watched as Honey-Lou squirmed on the table, and he imagined he could see the faintest ray of light shining out from her pussy.

Honey-Lou cried out with a terrifying shriek, and Colton heard the muffled *pop* sound as the light bulb imploded inside her. Blood began to trickle out of her cunt and pool on the table.

"Oh, hi Colton!" Eric bounded through the crowd. "Is it your turn now?"

"Err, no." Colton was taken aback. "You go right ahead, be my guest."

Eric leapt onto the table with a cursory hello to Honey-Lou and slipped his dick inside her with a pained howl and a squirt of blood.

Colton had no desire to watch his dog/son fuck Honey-Lou. Not that he was jealous or anything, it was just that he felt kind of ambivalent about the whole scene. This was quite possibly due to him growing weary of the dream, and he wished he could just wake the fuck up, or the fact that he had just cum all over Honey-Lou's butt. Either way, he decided to tuck his dick back into his pants and make his retreat.

***

Back in the atrium, as far as the eye could see, there were naked, writhing, fucking bodies in every combination possible, and some Colton had thought would be impossible. He stepped over and around the sweating, grunting, screaming people eager to be away from the assault on his senses the orgy now presented.

Colton was ready for the dream to come to an end, and he hoped he would be allowed to wake up before it all became too much for him here. The sexual excesses of the Resistance fighters had taken on a somewhat sinister, violent turn for Colton's liking, and he was ready to leave all of that behind, no matter what surprises Zeenah had waiting for him at the hospital.

And then, as he sidestepped a young couple who lay on the floor in a post-coital embrace, Colton realized they were dead. They were curled up in each others arms; her head was upon his chest and her unmoving eyes dry, staring into his.

And they weren't the only ones.

His heart racing, Colton looked over the orgy with fresh eyes and saw a great many of the participants that he thought were resting between activities were in fact dead. Many were frozen in their embraces like the couple at his feet, whilst some were twisted, broken, and bleeding from vicious assaults. Those that were still alive were fucking, beating, biting, and choking, as if keen to meet their own demise as quickly as possible.

A hand reached out for Colton and grabbed his ankle. He looked down into the imploring eyes of a gray-haired old woman. She was dragged away from him by two men who pulled her legs apart and rammed an impossibly large, wooden phallus into her. She screamed as she split wide open, and the men rubbed their dicks in her blood.

Colton began to run, no longer caring who or what he stepped on. He aimed himself toward the main door as he just wanted to be out of the place and away from the obscenity, the screams, and the stink. His feet skidded on a puddle of blood, and he fell face forward on to a tangled heap of people. Those couples on top were still alive; those beneath having had the life crushed from them. The top couples fucked frantically on their corpse bed, and their hands explored the bodies of the dead beneath them.

He struggled to his feet and continued on. Ahead of Colton, the main door opened, and he stopped in his tracks.

"Alicia," Colton cried out.

Alicia Forshay walked into the orgy accompanied by President Ocelot, who walked a few steps ahead of her.

Alicia was naked and had a lascivious smile that played across her lips.

"Hello, Colton," she said.

As Alicia made her way toward him, Colton couldn't help but take in that sexy sway of the hips, the slight bounce of her full breasts, the subtle pout of her pussy lips, and he felt the all too familiar stirring in his crotch again. No matter that his walking, talking wife was nothing more than an illusion created by the president, Colton wanted to take her any way he could right now.

And why not? This was *his* dream, after all.

Alicia reached out for her husband and circled her arms around his neck. She pulled his lips toward hers, parting them against Colton's with her tongue eager and probing. She dug her fingers into Colton's hair and pressed his face so hard into hers that he struggled to breathe. And then her hands were away from his hair and at his pants, which slid around his ankles in the blink of an eye.

Alicia pulled her husband to the floor and lay him down in the narrow space between a pair of dead girls, and Colton could feel their cold, clammy skin on his. Alicia straddled him and lowered her pussy onto his erection guiding it inside with her hand.

Colton let out a groan as Alicia's body closed around him, and for the first time in a long time, he felt fulfilled.

"This is number five," Alicia said. "Make sure you enjoy it."

"Eh?" Colton grunted.

"I'm afraid it's what you get when you gate crash one of my Devil's Roulette soirees," Alicia replied with a peculiar tone to her voice, and Colton realized he wasn't talking to, or fucking, *per se*, his wife. It was President Ocelot.

As if to emphasise that very point, the president came around to sit by Colton's head.

Colton struggled to get up, but Alicia held him firm with her hands on his chest, and her strong thighs around his hips.

"Don't fight it, Colton my darling, enjoy," Alicia instructed. She squeezed his penis with rhythmic pulses of her internal muscles, in effect, masturbating him with her vagina. "As I was forced to inform your former leader, the myth that the Roulette drug lasts for twelve hours is just that," the president told Colton through Alicia's voice. "For those of you unfortunate enough to have it administered, it lasts a lifetime."

"You're lying," Colton grunted. Despite himself, he could feel his orgasm as it raced toward him.

"Sadly, no, my friend," the president said, and Alicia shook her head. Colton thought he saw a hint of sadness in her eyes.

"I guess it doesn't really matter that much anyways." Colton laughed. "I'll be awake and out of this godforsaken dream before you know it."

"Then you may as well enjoy fucking your wife one last time." The president laughed along. "And while you do, let me tell you something about dreams."

Alicia's vaginal muscles rippled over Colton's cock like a thousand magical fingers. She held the rest of her body perfectly still, only her mouth moved with the president's words.

"There are some Native American tribes who believe a man exists in two states," the president continued. Each word, each breath was translated into a pleasurable tightening of Alicia's cunt on Colton's throbbing dick. "There is the daytime state, and the nighttime, or dream state."

By this point, Colton could only manage a grunt by means of reply.

"Their legends say a man can never be sure as to which is real, and which is the dream," the president said. All the while, he manipulated Alicia's body to intensify its pleasurable pressures on Colton.

"This *is* just a dream," Colton gasped. "I'm not fucking stupid."

"I'm not saying you are stupid, Colton," the president said, and his tail flicked as if swatting at a troublesome insect. "And you are quite right about it being just a dream. What I am saying, however, is that *this* is not your dream."

"That's bullshit," Colton groaned. His orgasm was close now, and he felt as if his insides were about to explode.

"I'm afraid not," the president said, and he made Alicia's mouth smile her sweetest smile. "For you, and all of the others like you who have dreamt of the other life, of money, love, and sex being only for recreation and procreation, of a place where sexual excess and debauchery are confined to the sick minority—that is little more than pathetic escapism."

Alicia stared down at Colton, and her eyes met his.

"Your world of white picket fences and cheating wives. That is the dream, Colton. This is your reality," she said. "Which is why we have to eliminate the Dreamers," the president continued. "And why I had to infiltrate the Resistance and put an end to it once and for all."

Colton shook his head and willed himself to wake up.

"It all leads to unrest; don't you see?" the president said. "We simply can't have any minority of the populace running against the crowd." Alicia's mouth upturned again. "Otherwise, we get this," she and the president looked around at the dead and the dying, at the ruined, bleeding bodies, the dead faces frozen in agony.

Colton tried once more to free himself from beneath Alicia. For as much as it went against his every instinct, he wanted to be out of Alicia's delightful pussy before he came.

Because if you die in your dream...

Unfortunately for Colton, his struggles only heightened the stimulation on his dick and brought him to wave after wave of intense orgasm. He closed his eyes and hoped to holy hell this wasn't his final cum.

"It looks like you were lucky," the president said as he peered between Alicia's legs. "This time."

"Fuck you," Colton snarled.

Alicia lifted herself off Colton, and he was intensely relieved to see his semen, and not blood, dribbled from her.

"Of course, that means that your next fuck *will* be your last fuck." The president laughed a light laugh. "Which would be a disaster, either way you care to look at it." The cat licked a paw. "If you refuse to believe me and still think this is the dream, then you die here, you die in what you think is your real life. And if you do believe me, and I think you might, Colton, if you die here, you die here." The president laughed through Alicia, mocking Colton with her happy, carefree sound.

Alicia lay herself down upon the floor beside Colton. She reclined against three of the most beautiful women in the orgy that were still alive, and they embraced her. Their exploring hands caressed her breasts, entwined their fingers down to her soaking wet sex and pulled her lips wide apart.

"You want more?" she/the president asked.

Colton looked over at his wife and thought that she had never looked so beautiful. His brain swirled and raced; he was confused by what the president had told him and desperate to believe he was being lied to, yet already beginning to doubt both his sanity and his very existence.

What if the damned cat was telling the truth? What if the place he considered his real world, complete with the cheating bitch Zeenah, was the dream, and *this* was his reality? A reality filled with sexual excess and warped fantasies in which his next fuck would mean death.

And what if it wasn't?

Colton was still rock hard and ached for Alicia, *his* Alicia, and he wanted nothing more than to be back inside her; to feel her vagina around his dick for what could well be one final time.

Colton maneuvered himself over Alicia, his dick aimed directly at her welcoming hole.

***

"He's waking up," the voice said.

"That's wonderful, Doctor," Zeenah's voice came through the darkness, its disappointment barely hidden.

Colton felt a gentle tugging on his eyelids as they removed the tape and light flooded into his eyes. He looked around and could see only fuzzy shapes as his eyes fought to adjust after so long in the blackness. He let out a sigh of relief. Cheating wife, hospital bed, and battered body aside, Colton couldn't have been more delighted to finally be awake and away from the horrific nightmares his mind had tormented him with.

"Take it easy, Mr. Forshay," the doctor's voice soothed. "You've been asleep for quite some time, so you are likely to experience some disorientation."

Colton tried to speak, but the tube in his throat kept him silent.

Then, as suddenly as it had appeared, the light began to fade, and Colton began to panic. A seeping grayness crept around the edges of his vision and closed in on the blurred shapes that stood around his hospital bed. Slowly, surely, the nebulous gray took away the light until all Colton could see was a blank block of thick, smothering gray.

And then the gray turned into black.

The voices spun away from Colton and faded into the blackness that was only getting darker.

And then Colton found he was wide awake.

***

Colton smiled at Alicia as he afforded his eyes the pleasure of soaking up the libertine beauty of her naked body. He held himself steady over his wife's cunt, his erection pointing out its intention.

"Welcome to the real world, Colton," President Ocelot greeted him. "Well, what *are* you going to do?"

The End

James H Longmore

ABOUT THE AUTHOR

James H. longmore hails originally from Doncaster, a mining town in the south of Yorkshire, Northern England; he relocated with his family to Houston, Texas in 2010. James boasts an honors degree in Zoology and a former career background in sales, marketing, and business.

He is an accomplished, published author (and publisher), and ghostwriter of popular fiction - he writes across a wide range of genres and subjects: novels, shorts, and screenplays. He has written and directed award-winning short movies, is an affiliate member of the Horror Writer's Association, and has run/hosted the popular podcast/radio show *The New Panic Room* since early 2016,

In addition, James is the founder and owner of the indie publisher, *HellBound Books Publishing LLC* (est. 2016), which publishes horror, bizarro, and a whole manner of dark fiction.

http://www.panicroomradio.com

http://www.hellboundbookspublishing.com/authorpage_longmore.html

ALSO BY JAMES H LONGMORE

BUDS

Wildus Guidry, amateur scientist extraordinaire, invents time travel. To his bitter disappointment, he discovers his device only transports him mere fractions of a second into the past. Inhabiting the new, alternate world of that fractional past is a variation of *Homo sapiens* that reproduce asexually by budding and uses sex as a recreational pastime and as a means of feeding. Disappointed by his discovery, Guidry and his entrepreneurial girlfriend decide to bring back some of the Buds and open the world's most bizarre and exclusive brothel - the Buds' unique appearance as grotesquely erotic conjoined twins, triplets, quadruplets (and more!) prove to be incredibly popular amongst the brothel's elite clientele. Of course, all goes terribly wrong as the Buds turn out to be not as benign as first thought, and chaos and the end of the world ensues.

Buds is a unique, sexy take on the popular time travel trope, and a must for all lovers of conjoined twin tales. An erotic, at times brutal and disturbing, story told with lashings of dark humor.

TENEBRION

"The Devil's in the detail."

Amateur filmmakers inadvertently invoke a demon when they break into an abandoned school to perform and film an authentic Black Mass for their entry into a short movie competition.

Dave Priestley and his crew film in Watsonville elementary school – the site of a horrific tragedy nine years before.

Tenebrion – the malevolent demon of darkness – makes preparations of its own within the dark recesses of Hell. The demon requires a specific set of circumstances and sacrifices to rend a fissure between the worlds and set free its brethren; it has manipulated humans for centuries to put things into place, and the moviemakers are the unfortunate, final pieces of its nefarious puzzle. Priestley, ever the stickler for authenticity and detail, accidentally sets free the denizen of Hell. And while Priestley and his skeptical friends attempt to return Tenebrion to the pit of Hades, it hunts them all down – one by one – for inclusion in its hellish gateway.

AND THEN YOU DIE:

Following a drunken, hedonistic night out in New Orleans, highly successful businesswoman and sexual deviant, Claire Jepson, accidentally soils herself in her car. The resulting excrement comes to life as a sardonic fecal spirit, and not only dishes out a gruesome death to Claire's unfaithful, gold-digging fiancé, but also thwarts a kidnap/murder plot by her employees. It then introduces Claire to a world of depraved pleasures beyond her imagination.

A year later, the errant spirit has spiraled wildly out of control - its insatiable appetite for perverted sex and human flesh and has destroyed Claire's life. Then, to her horror, Claire discovers the fecal spirit must consume her unborn child to attain immortality; she must return to the seedy underbelly of the Big Easy in a heart-pounding race against time to confront the spirit's creator - a high priest of an ancient, deadly order, who is the only one who can put a stop to the spirit's murderous intentions. A wicked, fast-paced story laced with tongue-in-cheek, dark humor, which is at the same time incredibly erotic and stomach churning. Most definitely not one to be read whilst eating!

PEDE:

An affectionate homage to the creature feature! The once luxurious Mountainview Spa Hotel in the heart of California's Coachella valley lies decaying, abandoned and heavily boarded up - the site of a radioactive, "dirty" bomb explosion five years' previously. Zoology Professor, Jane Lucas, harbors a lifelong phobia of *Scolopendra gigantea,* the Giant Centipede, despite being the world's leading authority on the creature. Following the savage deaths of two teenagers who broke into the hotel to cavort in the natural underground spa and the discovery of centipede remains almost three times natural size, the professor teams up with four of her students to investigate.

Their expedition soon becomes a fight for survival when they're trapped inside the hotel with a gang of violent thugs and a voracious swarm of oversized centipedes that infest the place - and then discover another creature even more terrifying is hunting in the Mountainview's deserted hallways: a centipede of impossibly monstrous proportions… ravenous and desperate to feed.

FLANAGAN

"The Devil's Rejects meets Fifty Shades – heart-pounding, gut-wrenching, sexy as all hell, and with a twist you'll never see coming!"

Meet the Sewells, an all-American couple; happily married for ten years, respected high school teachers, still crazy about one another, and with a mutually-shared dark side.

During their annual Spring Break vacation to recharge batteries and reconnect, the Sewells are waylaid by a perverse gang of misfits in the one-horse, North Texas town of Flanagan.

Taken hostage to be the focus of the gang's twisted games, the Sewells are brutalized into performing vicious physical, sexual, and emotional acts upon one another, until events take an unexpected turn, triggered by an unintentional death. As their circumstances descend into the worse nightmare imaginable, the Sewells find themselves involved in an altogether different situation...

BLOOD AND KISSES

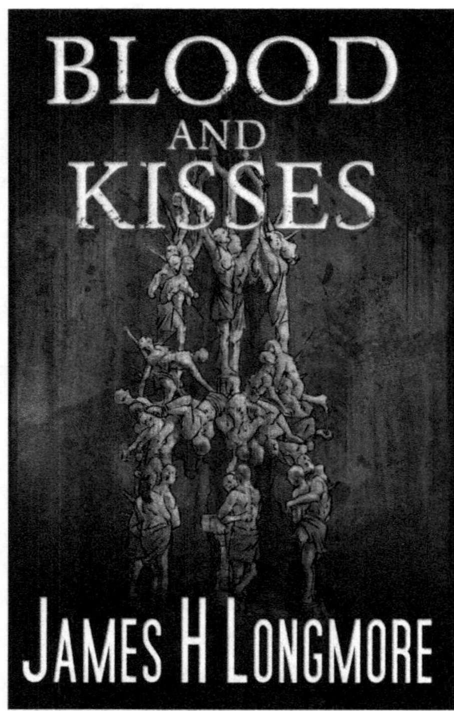

"Think of what late greats James Herbert and Richard Laymon may have given birth to had they ever collaborated"
- Richard Chizmar
The definitive short story collection from James H Longmore - an eclectic mix of dark horror, bizarro and *Twilight Zone* style tales of the downright disturbing.
Welcome to the long-awaited collection from the writer of horror novels *'Pede* and *Tenebrion*; a foreword by Richard Chizmar (co-author of *Gwendy's Button Box* with Stephen King), 18 short stories, 5 flash fiction, and a poem - all skin-crawling, soul-shredding tales of the darkest things that skulk among the night's inky shadows and of the everyday gone horribly awry.
Discover the implication of technology becoming self-aware, enjoy the acquaintance of a charismatic new pastor promising his flock a brand new place to worship his God, spend a little time in the company of a nice young man who is inexorably caught up in his home town's terrible secret.
Then, there's Cupid's revelation he's never experienced love, we discover that very emotion alive and not so well

among the ruins of a post-zombie apocalyptic world, and bear witness to childhood innocence forever destroyed in a distant, war-torn city.

Observe, too any unsavory individual's obsession with the ever-elusive snuff movie, and join an elderly bunch of forgetful sleuths out to solve the mystery of brutal deaths that occur with alarming regularity at their memory care facility.

Now, have you ever considered what may happen should you have the misfortune to bump into your family's doppelgangers on a long, tedious road trip? And, can you even begin to imagine being the doting father who finally realizes the apple of his eye's true identity, or the parents who spend what is left of their crumbling lives waiting by a silent telephone for news of their addict son?

There is more, Dear Reader, much, much more; for within the pages we have devils, demons and ghosts, lycanthropes, and demi-gods, all rubbing nefarious shoulders with the most vile of Hell's offspring, who have slithered up from the netherworld to doff their caps and wish us all the sweetest of dreams…

FEEDER

A deliciously bizarro, darkly disturbing peek into the world of gainers and feeders: grotesquely obese individuals and those people who facilitate their growth for the lascivious pleasure of both parties.

The heroine of the piece, Novella, Embarks upon a journey into the dreadful netherworld that dwells within the obese, fleshy folds of a woman especially engorged for the perverted delights of her Internet audience. Aided and abetted by a former feeder, she fights to escape before the grim portal closes and she's trapped forever in the ghastly realm of fat, flesh, and death most gruesome.

<u>I AM JOE'S UNWANTED PENIS</u>

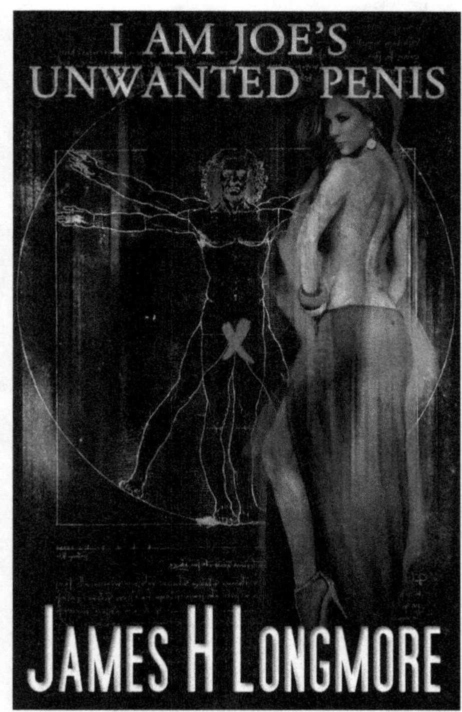

A darkly comedic tribute to the much-loved Reader's Digest series *'I am Joe's…(insert body part here)'* and a bizarre parody of the Bruce Jenner story, *I Am Joe's Unwanted Penis* is told from the point of view of a penis discarded as a man is surgically transformed into a woman.

Upon learning if his high-profile previous owner's regret at having made the transformation, the penis embarks upon a perilous journey for them to be reunited - aided and abetted by a motley, wonderfully personable, and engaging selection of other discarded body parts.

In parts grotesque, laugh-out-loud funny, and undeniably poignant, in others, *I Am Joe's Unwanted Penis* is a buddy-story absolutely like no other!

**A HellBound Books LLC
Publication 2021**

www.hellboundbookspublishing.com

Printed in the United States of America